THE CRYSTAL PLANETOIDS

By
STANTON A. COBLENTZ

ARMCHAIR FICTION
PO Box 4369, Medford, Oregon 97504

For more information about Armchair Books and products, visit our website at…

www.armchairfiction.com

Or email us at…

armchairfiction@yahoo.com

THE DAY THE EARTH STARTED TO GET HOT

It was first thought to be just an unusually hot season—high temperatures and little wind. But when the same freakish weather conditions appeared to be happening all over the Earth, the scientific community knew there was something disastrous afoot. A great, foggy haze seemed to settle over the entire planet. Every day temperatures shot up into the hundreds— all over the entire planet. Thousands died.

It was only a chance discovery by a scientific inventor that revealed the Earth was under attack, and the invading marauders came from the planet Saturn. Using a complex maze of invisible webs, the Saturnian invaders were slowly turning the Earth into a hell-house. From their orbiting Crystal Planetoids above, it appeared they had only to wait a little longer for all life on Earth to perish.

FOR A SECOND COMPLETE NOVEL, TURN TO PAGE 111

CAST OF CHARACTERS

RONALD GATES
This brilliant scientific tinkerer invented a new infra-red viewing device, but what he discovered with it defied scientific reality.

PHILIP DUNBAR
There was no question that when the going got tough, he was more interested in saving his own skin than anything else.

ELEANOR FIRTH
She had a fair sense of women's intuition, but ignoring it got her into a dangerous situation that might end up costing her life!

THE PEERLESS RED ONE
He was an intelligent but decidedly cruel tyrant from the planet Saturn—and his sights were now set on Earth.

POLICE CHIEF JOE McCULLOUGH
He'd been around a long time and knew how to handle all sorts of characters, including crazy ladies with tales of invading aliens.

MISTHRUMB
This yellow-clawed alien was the would-be killer of the Peerless Red One—a desire that brought him far more than he expected.

CHAPTER ONE
The New Invention

PHILIP DUNBAR ran a lean exploratory hand through his tousled long black hair. There was a sardonic, faintly quizzical look in his dark, trimly moustached face, which acquaintances were inclined to describe as "handsome, but saturnine." His little jet-points of eyes, as he stared across at the next laboratory table, glittered enigmatically.

"Well, Ronny," he inquired, in a drawl that rasped, "found it at last?"

Ronald Gates peered up from amid a mass of lenses, batteries and wires. His frank, open face widened into a broad smile. His clear blue eyes sparkled.

"Yes, by heaven," he confessed, enthusiastically, "I think I've got that devil licked."

Instantly Dunbar was at his side.

"Like hell you have!" he doubted.

At the same time, from the opposite end of the great laboratory, a feminine voice broke out.

"Oh, good, Ronald, I knew you'd do it." And the tall form of Eleanor Firth, its youthful attractiveness scarcely dimmed by the stained rubber gloves and apron she was wearing, came gliding toward the men. Her big golden-brown eyes blazed with admiration as she turned them full upon Gates. "I knew it, Ronald—I knew you simply had to!"

To an onlooker, the relationship of the men and the girl would have been crystal-clear. Dunbar's manner, as he glared at Gates, was dagger-sharp; Gates had no eyes for Dunbar at all; while both men regarded the young lady with softening glances that were eloquent.

Why was it, Dunbar reflected, that they had all taken to staying in overtime here at their place of employment, the laboratory of the Merlin Research Institute? True, Gates was all worked up about that damnable invention of his! And Eleanor—wasn't it just like a woman to find an excuse to stay when she knew Gates would be there? As for himself—if he didn't want to be shoved out of the picture, he had no choice but to work on after hours.

"Yes, by glory, I think I've done the trick!" Gates was exclaiming. "If you folk'll just come with me to the roof, I'll demonstrate…"

He took up a black instrument resembling a pair of opera glasses, except that it was equipped with large red lenses, and was attached by wires to a cluster of minute batteries and radio-like tubes.

"What did you say you call the contraption?" asked Dunbar, as Gates started upstairs with his invention.

"The Infra-Red Eye."

"Why in blazes do you call it that?"

"Just wait a minute, and you'll see. You know as well as I do, Dunbar, photographs taken in infra-red light will reveal clear details through a mist. Why must the human eye be blind where the camera can see? It is all a question of securing the proper adaptation to etheric vibrations—which I have done by means of invisible rays produced by electrical action on certain iridium and osmium salts in these tubes."

DUNBAR grunted a half coherent reply, and threw open the roof-door. As they carne out into the heavy mist-laden air of the late July afternoon, the humidity rolled from them visibly. There was a peculiar stagnation in the atmosphere, as though the very breath of heaven had been congealed. Featureless gray clouds hung wearily over the landscape; a dull, blank haze obscured everything beyond a few hundred yards. One might have said that—" the very elements had gone to sleep.

"Goodness, I do wish we could get some relief from this atrocious heat," sighed Eleanor.

"The twenty-ninth continuous day of it, unless I've missed my count," grumbled Dunbar, as he mopped his perspiring brow. "Doesn't it beat the devil? What's more, it's getting worse!"

"Yes, and the strangest thing of all is, it seems to affect the whole world!" returned the girl. "I just can't believe it's not something more than common weather…"

"Hate to tell you what I suspect it is," returned Dunbar, ominously.

"Come, come, folks, what are you so cheerful about, all of a sudden?" Gates demanded, as he examined the adjustments of the wires. "Good heavens…I'm sick and tired of hearing there's something supernatural about a heat spell, just because it happens to be unusually prolonged."

"Yes, but the other phenomenal," broke in Dunbar, his sharp eyes glinting with hostility. "The dust clouds—the checking of normal wind movements—the indefinable thickening in the atmosphere—the thunder storms of unprecedented violence—"

"Nothing has been definitely established," denied Gates. "Personally, I doubt if it's anything at all, aside from a cycle of exceptional sun-spot activity. But we're wasting our time. Ready now for the infra-red eye?"

"I'm all keyed up!" announced Eleanor, casting the young man one of her strangely kindled, animated glances.

"Here, you make the first test," he decided, thrusting the black instrument into her hands. "Just fit it to your eyes like binoculars. Turn that screw for the adjustment. Wait! I'll see to the current…"

He switched a lever, drew back a panel, and pressed a button. But, aside from a faint whirring sound, there was no apparent effect.

"Now focus the instrument," he went on. "Point it anywhere. If you don't see through that haze as easily as a knife cuts butter; then set me down as a fraud and a liar!"

The girl screwed up her eyes. Faint wrinkles were visible on her broad, creamy white brow. A second passed in silence. Then an astonishing change overcame her countenance.

All at once, her lips drew apart in an incredulous expression. A gasp came from between her lips. A pallor spread across her cheeks. For several seconds she remained as if glued to the instrument.

GRIMACING wryly, she snapped herself away from the eye-piece with a horrified "Ugh!" Her eyes bulged. Her whole form was trembling.

"I—I—I guess I'm seeing things!" she explained, lamely.

Then, observing how strangely Dunbar was staring at her, she thrust the instrument at him.

"Here, you—you just look for yourself!"

Dunbar took up the apparatus, and peered through it steadily for perhaps half a minute. But he too, when he put it down, was visibly paler.

"Am I crazy?" he grunted. "Here, Ronny, better have a peep yourself—"

But Gates had already snatched up the instrument. And he too gasped as he adjusted the lenses. For he saw nothing that he had anticipated.

The only purpose of the Infra-Red Eye, as he himself had declared, had been to penetrate a haze. But how startlingly the results had exceeded expectations!

Spread far above the Earth's surface, in the form of colossal cobwebs, were long tenuous strands, woven in a web many layers deep. The threads, colorless and almost transparent, were thin as though composed of some silken fabric; but were enormously long, and stretched in great curves from horizon to zenith. Over the entire firmament they seemed to be bent and twisted by the tens of thousands, forming intricate geometric patterns, and uncannily giving the impression of enclosing the Earth in a great cage. Wavering slightly in the faint breezes of the upper spaces, they covered every section of the visible heavens, even spreading their dim crisscrossing bars across the moon.

As if this discovery in and of itself was not ghastly enough, a still more terrible sight presented itself. Scores of beings, vaguely human-shaped and each with many limbs dangling octopus-like, swung agilely along the gigantic webs. Of prodigious size—seemingly not less than fifteen or twenty feet tall—the creatures were of a watery pallor that made only the bare outlines of their forms visible. Each, in the middle of an egg-shaped head, displayed two oddly three-cornered eyes that glowed with dull red flames; each possessed six or eight many-fingered hands with which it was adding new segments to the monstrous web.

With a groan, Gates put down the instrument; and, wiping his streaming brow, sagged against a wall for support. But the horror in his eyes matched that in the faces of his companions as the three stared at one another in openmouthed amazement.

CHAPTER TWO
The Terror Strikes

IT WAS as Dunbar had remarked. For nearly a month, unexampled meteorological disturbances had been occurring throughout the Earth. Not only in the northern hemisphere had a record heat blanketed every land; in regions far below the Equator, the accustomed mid-winter chill had disappeared; indeed, an almost tropical calm had been reported as far south as Cape Horn. Everywhere on the Earth's surface, normal wind currents had been retarded or halted; everywhere dust and mist had accumulated; everywhere—even in the usually thunderless coastal regions of California—electrical storms of unparalleled violence had been of almost daily occurrence. But scientists, having no plausible explanation, had for the most part looked on in mute bewilderment.

There were, however, some who professed to believe that the shattered remnants of a comet had entered the Earth's atmosphere; and supported their theory by pointing out that quantities of some gaseous foreign substance, which as yet they had been unable to analyze, had been detected in the stratosphere; while scores of high-flying airplanes had recently been slowed down or wrecked by unexplained impediments.

Few persons as yet saw any connection between the extraordinary weather and the reports of astronomers that dozens of minute bodies had been detected through telescopes, revolving as satellites about the Earth just beyond its atmospheric limits. For lack of a better theory, it was assumed that they were asteroids or "minor planets" which had ventured too close to the Earth and had been caught by its gravitational power; although no one could say why so many of them should have been discovered almost simultaneously. Besides, it was hard to account for the peculiar glassy appearance of these so-called Crystal Planetoids—an appearance, which did not at all indicate the nickel, or iron composition that might have been expected.

NOT all these facts were in the minds of the three observers on the roof as they made their disconcerting discovery. But there were certain things that they did realize clearly enough.

"By glory," exclaimed Gates, his big eyes as wide with surprise as though he had seen the dead. "By glory! I just can't believe those great spidery devils are real—"

"Real or not, I—I've got a feeling we shouldn't stay here," Eleanor muttered, her face still white, as she started toward the door. "I—I—something tells me it isn't safe!"

"What in tarnation do you think can happen to us here more than down below?" demanded Gates. And then, with a shrug, "I'm going to take another peep through that glass."

"Sure, go ahead. Might as well all wait, and die together!" Dunbar growled. "D'ya know, I've got an idea Eleanor's right. If we've a spark of sense left in our hides—"

Gates cast him a scornful glance, noting what an abject figure he seemed to be, as, with terror convulsing his lean, moustached face, he went slouching away.

"Hope I'll fall dead before I get so soft," reflected the inventor.

Yet, despite himself, his pulses were throbbing as he returned to the Infra-Red Ray and observed the ominous, ruddy glow that, within the last minute, had come across the heavens. Was not the atmosphere thicker, hotter, heavier than ever? Why did it seem to bear down on him like a stony weight? Why within him that impulse which he sternly repressed—that impulse to race for shelter?

For a few seconds, after he had readjusted the instrument, he saw only what he had observed before: the prodigious spidery webs, with the huge octopus-limbed creatures swinging across them.

But almost immediately he made another observation. And, as he did so, a cry came to his lips. It was a cry of horror, issuing from some vast instinctive depth—a cry such as one might utter if one saw a man-eating tiger springing toward one with wide-open jaws. "For God's sake! Quick! Run—for your lives!"

Even as he uttered this plea, Gates dropped the instrument and started away. Dunbar was already in the doorway, into which he was disappearing with the violence of panic; while just behind him Eleanor was scampering like a frightened wild thing.

But they were just a second too late. There came a rushing as of a great wind. There came a moment as of immense shadows, sweeping down with lightning velocity. There came a glimpse of tenuous shapes in rapid motion, a little like the spokes of a furiously turning wheel. At the same time, in a nightmarish, unbelievable fashion, Gates saw Dunbar and Eleanor arrested in mid-flight. Something vague and gray, which looked like a gigantic claw, seemed to be woven about them both. But it all happened too quickly for him to be sure. In the same instant, he beheld them both jerked into air; then whirled skyward at rocket speed, while their cries rang in his ears.

At the same instant also, as he stared at his companions, stunned and gasping, he felt something soft but powerful seizing him about the middle—something wriggling, and snake-like, and icy chill of touch. He was never to know whether he screamed in the extremity of his terror; all that he was aware was that there came a mighty jerk, and that, helpless as a hare in an eagle's talons, he rose into air with a speed that almost beat out his breath; and saw the roofs of the city fading beneath him amid the reddish haze.

FOR several minutes, beneath the clubbing rapidity of the flight, the captive's senses deserted him. And when, feeling dazed and drugged, he revived, it was to find himself amid a universe of fog in which the Earth had receded from sight. He had, however, the distinct sensation of still rising—rising at tremendous speed. And he noticed—and this, to his mind, was the most incredible thing of all—that he was surrounded by an egg-shaped jelly-like transparent envelope about fifteen feet long. Not until much later did he realize that this envelope enclosed oxygen enough for him to breathe, and maintained it at a temperature and pressure without which life at his great elevation would have been impossible.

He had no way of knowing how much time went by in that nightmarish flight. He did, however, feel sure that many minutes had passed before at length he found himself above the mists. Blanketed in vapor, the Earth rolled beneath him, shadowy and featureless; while, in a crepuscular dimness, he saw the stars glittering from the purple-gray void. But what particularly held his attention was the sight of several monstrous creatures—long and spidery, and with dangling octopus limbs—which drifted ghost-like through the vagueness just outside the egg-shaped envelope, with malevolently glowing three-cornered reddish eyes.

As he still rose, past what might have been the upper limits of the stratosphere, he saw a silvery globe sparkling above him in the moonlight. At first he thought it to be a mere speck; but its disk rapidly widened, until it appeared as large as the sun, then as great as several suns, then seemed to fill the entire heavens with its pale glassy form, which shed a tintless cold light that made Gates shudder.

Actually, the sphere was not more than a few hundred yards across; but to the bewildered victim it seemed enormous as some prodigy of nature. His confusion was only increased by the fact that he saw the stars moving rapidly past it, with a westward drift, showing that it was swinging swiftly to the east on an orbit of its on. So dazed was the captive that it took him minutes to identify it as one of the Crystal Planetoids.

By this time, they had reached the surface of the sphere, which he could see to be composed of a jelly-like substance with the appearance of milky glass. As they drew near, their speed rapidly diminished, until they came to a halt almost in contact with the great globe. Then, as if at its own volition, part of the surface billowed back, like a paper flap blown by the wind; and Gates, with the sensation of one entering a prison in a strange land, found himself drifting inside the sphere.

As suddenly as if it had evaporated, the egg-shaped envelope had disappeared, and he caught a whiff of hot, heavy, foul-smelling air, reminding him of a breeze straight from a menagerie. He coughed and gasped, and, as he did so, became aware of an unimaginably horrifying scene.

HE STOOD inside the sphere at its lowest part, and gazed up into a circular space that, to his startled senses, seemed of stupendous magnitude. Woven about this vastness at all heights and angles was an intricacy of webs; webs built in concentric circles; webs composed of long parallel cables crisscrossed by shorter cables; webs ascending as sharply as the riggings of sailing vessels; and webs spun into hammock-like floating platforms. All the strands were thinner than a man's small finger, and shimmered strangely in the many-hued fluorescence of great light-patches on the ceiling; and somehow their iridescence, their shifting rainbow hues, their purples, ambers, aqua-marines, scarlets and turquoise blues, made them seem all the stranger and more sinister.

But most sinister of all were the great beings sprinting along the webs or dangling spider-like from a thread. Now for the first time Gates saw his captors clearly; for now— as he was later to learn—they had brushed off the powder that made them virtually invisible to human eyes, and stood forth in their full grotesqueness.

Their outlines were what he had already seen: gigantic, spidery, with octopus limbs ending in many tentaclelike curling fingers. He had not known, however, that the monsters were encased in a scaly armor, which glittered with every peacock hue in the unearthly light, changing chameleon-like from ruby to emerald, and from gold and violet to bronze, jade and sulphur-yellow. He had not known that they had wide pouting greenish-gray lips, from which at times a faint smoke issued. He had not realized that they were equipped with long whips of tails, each ending in a horny dart, with which they could strike an enemy with appalling effect. He had not anticipated that they would talk with a peculiar whirr, a little like the grating of a buzz-saw; nor had he expected to see the pouches beneath their lower ribs, in which some of them, kangaroo-fashion, carried their young.

Scarcely had Gates been deposited in the Planetoid when he made still an, other discovery.

"Great heavens, look at Ronald!" he heard a familiar feminine voice. And, wheeling about, he found himself staring at Dunbar and Eleanor, who gaped at him not half a dozen yards away.

Both were, literally, as white as ghosts—wide-eyed as persons who have looked on unmentionable horror. Gates noticed that Dunbar's hair, usually so sleekly glossed, straggled in wild disorder; that his tie was a rag, and his coat buttons torn off as if in a struggle; while Eleanor's clothes were in rumpled disorder. Yet he noted with relief that neither captive, apparently, had been hurt.

"Thank God!" the girl explained. "You're whole and sound!"

"Even if a little mussed up," Dunbar forced out, with a wry grimace. "Good Lord! Why, his shirt is in ribbons! And his collar—"

But he was not to finish the sentence. For Gates suddenly cried out, with a sensation as if a boa constrictor had seized him about the chest. One of the monsters, its red eyes glaring balefully, had reached down and grasped him in its tentacles; and, with the manner of a master reprimanding a disobedient puppy, had begun to carry him away.

CHAPTER THREE
Red-Hood

STRAIGHT up and up a swinging ladder the prisoner was borne for scores of yards; while, as he gazed into the abyss and thought of the result if his captor's hold should slacken, his head reeled with vertigo.

But his terror was not for himself alone. Even as he was hurtled high in air, he glanced down and saw an octopus' arm wrapping itself about a feminine form. And fury and alarm for Eleanor's sake drowned out all self-concern. In a flash, as his persecutor wound his way through the webbed void; he relived the history of his acquaintance with Eleanor. He saw again that day, little more than a year ago, when she, fresh from college, had come to the laboratory; and recalled the great leap his heart had given, and how he had gone away thinking only of her. But a natural timidity had delayed his advances; while Dunbar, the silent, morose Dunbar, whom nobody liked, had not been so restrained. Could she not see that the man, though clever enough, was as self-centered as a porcupine? How could she have fallen for this schemer? Not that she had fallen for him absolutely! Though they had been seen together frequently, was she not always gracious to Gates? Yet the rivalry of the two men was bubbling way beneath the surface like acid.

These thoughts, which passed through Gates mind in much less time than it takes to repeat them, were interrupted by a peculiar squeal which his captor gave out as he reached one of the hammock-like floating platforms and released the victim. Clinging to this unsteady island high in air, an imminent peril of plunging into a two-hundred-foot gulf, the prisoner was not likely to attempt escape!

But even had there been anywhere to flee, he would have been held by the magnetism of a particularly large, sinister-looking pair of crimson eyes, which glowed from a monster who appeared, to Gates' startled gaze, to be at least twenty-five feet tall. A blood-red hood, placed upon the creature's many-hued mail, set him off from all his fellows; as did the air of autocratic command which, somehow, Gates sensed rather than observed directly.

While he stood gaping at this goblin, a sharp cry to his left caught his attention; and, wheeling about, he observed Eleanor and Dunbar being deposited at his side. Both were trembling, as well they might, after their journey up the web, but he thought he saw a glint of relief in the girl's eyes, as he gestured to her.

A long, portentous silence fell as the red-hooded brute glared at his victims. Gates had the sensation of standing before a judge about to pass sentence of execution.

Then there came a throaty rumbling, followed by a buzzing as of a multitude of bees; after which, to the hearers' incredulous amazement, these words rasped forth, in grossly accented yet quite recognizable English.

"Welcome, my guests! Welcome to our web!"

THE three humans stared at one another, their lips agape. Had they all gone crazy?

The red eyes of the beast gave a wicked twinkle. Somehow, with their triangular scarlet pupils; they seemed more diabolical than ever.

"Come, come, do you not return my greeting?" buzzed the creature; while a grating noise, which may have been laughter, came from his companions.

"How—how in thunder do you come to speak English?" sputtered Gates, feeling that he was but living through a nightmare from which he would soon awaken.

Again that grating noise, like harsh laughter.

"English—pooh! It is not hard to learn. It is not as if it were an advanced language," proceeded Red-Hood. "But you Earthlings, with your minor-planetary minds, may not understand. Do you want me to explain?"

"Why not?" gasped Gates. But had he not steadied himself barely in time, he might have fallen off the platform.

"Well, it is all so very simple," went on the monster. "When arriving here, we covered ourselves with the powder Amvol-Amvol, which makes us invisible, or almost so. We then roamed your planet for many days, unseen by you, observing your habits, and listening to your conversations. Not being slow-witted like Earth denizens, we were able to pick up the meaning of the words, which we held in our memories—memories that register every thing, and never forget. After all, it is not for nothing that we are gifted with Saturnian intellects."

"Saturnian?" demanded Dunbar.

"Yes, that is the word you would use, is it not? We come from the planet Olar-olargulu, the ringed one."

The hearers remained silent. After all, it had been evident from the first that the strangers had not been born on Earth!

"This is our first experience with the inferior globules," continued the speaker, in a voice like a growl. We have never before spoken with any of you Negnegs, or lesser peoples. But of late centuries we of Saturn have become too numerous, even for the great size of our native planet. So we have been looking for provinces to colonize. For various reasons, we have chosen the Earth. As for Mars— it is too small to bother with. Jupiter, unfortunately, is too powerfully defended by its three-footed dwarfs. And Venus is too near the sun for comfort. So we are prepared to take over the Earth."

"Take over—the Earth?" demanded the three humans, in one voice.

"What else? After all, are we not entitled to it, by virtue of our superior intelligence?"

HIS hearers could merely stare in bewildered silence.

"Our method, you see, is simple. We have ferried these cars—which you call the Crystal Planetoids—all the way from Saturn, and placed them in positions to whirl about the Earth as satellites, enabling us to drop down upon our future domains at leisure, while weaving our clogclotlas—"

"Your what?" demanded Gates.

"Pardon me," apologized Red-Hood, while a spout of smoke came from between his thick grayish-green lips, and his tail lashed out and shot its hornet dart to within half a dozen inches of the young man's face. "Pardon me—I had forgotten myself, and used a Saturnian term. Weaving our webs, I should have said. You see, it is necessary to spin these webs thoroughly through your entire atmosphere before choking out all the planet's native life."

The speaker had made this announcement in as quiet a manner as though he had merely foretold that tomorrow's weather would be rainy.

Hence his hearers were hardly able to take in his full dread meaning. They merely gaped at him as though he were perpetrating a ghastly joke.

"What! Do you doubt me?" rattled out the monster. "Beware lest I take offense! We Saturnians never lie to our inferiors."

This assertion was punctuated by another flick of the creature's tail, whose rapier-like barb barely missed Dunbar's nose.

"But you don't mean to say you would actually exterminate us—exterminate us all—" began Eleanor; then faltered, and halted in confusion.

"Why not? Would you Earth-creatures hesitate to wipe out a hive of ants? Doubtless they too have minds, and even a civilization of a sort. But what is that to you? If they got in your way, would you not crush them?"

"So we are no more to you than ants?"

"Do not flatter yourselves. Why should we be sentimentalists, and spare you negnegs unless you can serve us?"

The puff of smoke that came from between the monster's lips, as he spat out these words, was so heavy that all three humans gasped, with the stench of sulphur in their nostrils.

"As I have said," he went on, "our clogclotlas, or webs, have been woven all through your atmosphere, checking the usual wind currents, and laying down a blanket that will enclose the planet's heat, until after a time every living creature will be baked or choked to death in one vast oven. Of course, like any other great engineering project, this will take time. We cannot expect to complete the good work in less than a year or two."

In Gates' disturbed fancy, it seemed that many-colored points of light, like little demons, danced malevolently upon the huge expanse of his captor's armor; Yet there was just a trace of incredulity in his tone, as he demanded.

"If this is all true, why do you trouble to tell us about it? We for our part do not warn the ants we intend to trample!"

"Nor do we!" Red-Hood's words came in a snort, and his tail flicked through the air in an angry crackling. "But whether we will spare you or sting you to death remains to be seen!"

THE beast took a sudden step forward, and Gates found himself almost projected off the platform as the monster shot out at him.

"Do you not think we brought you to the Planetoid for a purpose? For a long while, have we not been looking for suitable Earth-captives? No, not at first members of the common pack! We wanted prisoners who knew something of your science, rudimentary as that is. When you went to the roof down there to use your ray machine—the Infra-Red Eye, as you call it—you set up etheric vibrations that instantly attracted our attention. Your ability to produce such vibrations told us that you were the folk we were seeking. So we lost no time about capturing you."

During the moment of silence that followed, Dunbar turned toward Gates with unveiled enmity in his snapping black eyes.

"So!" he snarled. "It was your damned invention that got us into this mess!"

Gates made no reply; but an answer came from an unexpected direction.

"You should thank him, Earth-man, for getting you into this mess. Because of his invention, you three may live while all other Earth-creatures perish."

"What in God's name would life on such terms be worth?" Gates demanded. But a sob to his left caught his attention; and, wheeling about, he joined Dunbar in trying to console the weeping girl.

With a contemptuous glint in his triangular eyes, Red-Hood stood looking on; but it was several moments before he resumed.

"Life is dear to all creatures—and you will find it not worthless on our terms."

"What are your terms?"

It was Dunbar who asked this question, while Gates felt a silent resentment against the other man leap up within him.

"They are really most reasonable," the monster announced, sliding back and forth on the web, while his scales clanked ominously. "You see, even after all we have done, we find it hard to work on Earth. The air is much too thin. After we have thickened the atmosphere with a complete network, things will be different; but as yet we labor under great disadvantages. What we need are tanks of compressed air to assist us at times with our breathing. Such compressed air can be much easier supplied by you Earth creatures. That is why we have captured you. And that is why we promise you your lives—if you will do us a little service."

Gates glared back at Red-Hood in unconcealed fury. That this creature, who was threatening to wipe out the human race, should ask for his assistance—the idea was too preposterous, too heinous for consideration! And he was glad to note, from the revulsion in Eleanor's face, that she felt no less shocked than he.

But it was in unbelief, swiftly turning to anger, that he heard Dunbar's low, even voice, inquire.

"And what little service do you want of us?"

The gray-green lips of the Saturnian opened in a hideous grin.

"I knew from the first," he rasped, "that you Earth-animals would be reasonable. Our proposition is simply this: we will release you all, on condition that, on your return to Earth, you prepare great containers of compressed air, according to our directions. If you do this faithfully, we will see that your lives are spared even after the extinction of all other Earth-creatures."

"And if we refuse?" demanded Gates.

Red-Hood took a menacing stride forward.

"You will not refuse!" he proclaimed, again with a puff of sulphur fumes. "For in that case you will suffer a fate a hundred times worse than death…"

With ominous rapidity, the monster's tail whipped out once more, flashing back and forth before all three captives. And Gates, edging again toward the webbed abyss, had a momentary idea of leaping over the brink. But even as this thought came to him, he felt an ice-cold arm lashing him in a firm grip. Harsh, loud and ironic, the monster's derision grated in his ears.

"Not yet, my friend, not yet! The road of escape will be long and spiky! The road of escape will be long and spiky for all who defy the will of Saturn!"

These words were emphasized by a peal of laughter, shrill, grating, diabolical, wherein all the on looking monsters joined in one prolonged scream.

CHAPTER FOUR
"Cooperate—and Live!"

"EARTH-MEN, we are not impatient! We know your minds work like rusty hinges—but what else can be expected of the minor planets? So take a little time. Consult with one another. We will allow you half an hour. Then we will be back, and learn if you prefer to cooperate—or to die a thousand deaths…"

With an agile looping movement, Red-Hood started down one of the cable ladders, followed by all his retinue.

"One thing more," he warned, noting how longingly Gates was staring into the abyss. "Take care not to fall off the platform. In that case, strong arms will be waiting to catch you—and your punishment will be heavy in proportion to the crime…"

"How heavy will that be?" defied Gates, wondering what they could do to him worse than they had already threatened.

Scarlet flashes shot from the monster's eyes. "One hundred of your kind," he snorted, "will be picked up from the streets of your cities, and crushed to death as hostages. Such is the vengeance of Saturn…"

As the creature left, with a low hissing as of escaping steam, Gates felt as never before that he was in contact with a force having nothing in common with humanity.

Silence ruled for a moment, while the three prisoners sat facing one another on their high swinging perch. But their horror-filled eyes were eloquent.

"God in heaven! I don't suppose there's much for us to decide," mumbled Gates grimly while he stared as in a nightmare at the looping, crisscrossing intricacy of cables overhead.

"No, I'm sure not," sighed Eleanor.

"Any idiot could see that," Dunbar muttered. "Don't know what we need this half hour to think about…"

Another gloomy silence ensued.

"Well, at least I'm glad we're agreed," declared Gates, who to tell the truth was a little surprised at Dunbar's sudden manifestation of decent feeling.

"Wouldn't we be imbeciles not to be," Dunbar drawled, running a lean, long-fingered hand reflectively across his jutting chin. "All comes down, I guess, to a question of saving our own hides. As for me—I never did exactly hanker to shine as a martyr."

"Martyr?" echoed Gates. And all at once he knew the full enormity of Dunbar's treason—yes, knew beyond all need for further questioning!

At the same time, he noticed Eleanor's nauseated look

"Damn it, Ronny, mean to say I got you wrong? So you folks are not with me after all?" demanded Dunbar, incredulously. "Deuce take you! I never thought you were that crazy."

"If you call it crazy not to betray your whole race—"

"I'd like to know what in hell my whole race has ever done for me!" retorted Dunbar. "Lot it'll help them if I let myself be ground to bits by those snaky dragons! No, sirree, you can play the saint if you want to—but I'll think you're both hell-blasted fools. As for me—I'll cooperate—and live…"

"I'd rather be a hell-blasted fool than live with the world's blood on my hands. Wouldn't you, Eleanor?"

"A thousand times over!" attested the girl. And in her animated eyes, as she nodded assent, there was a warmth. Gates hadn't observed in them before.

"You're letting your feelings rule you, Ronny, not your mind," swore Dunbar. "That's the trouble with you—too infernal much of a dreamer. Can't face reality. Why, haven't I seen it in you all along? You haven't got the guts of a jellyfish. That's why I've despised you!"

THERE it was out in the open again, their antagonism flaring white-hot. Somehow it seemed strange, ludicrous that the three of them should be perched here, on the rim of eternity as it were, and be doing nothing better than air their personal enmities. Yet, after all, did Gates not know that Dunbar had always loathed him?

It was Eleanor's voice that broke the brief, bristling silence. Struggling to gain control of herself, she cast a defiant glance at Dunbar. "You are badly mistaken, Philip!" she defended, crisply, "if you think Ronald hasn't got, as you say, the guts of a jellyfish. I guess it doesn't take so much guts to be a traitor, the way you're planning, Mr. Dunbar! And let us both die while you go pleasantly along your way!"

Tears were in the girl's eyes; she had to avert her face violently to prevent a telltale overflow.

Dunbar's answer was a low, gruff laugh.

"Good Lord...what makes you think I'm willing to let you both die? Ronny...can do what he damn well wants to...guess the world will outlive his loss. But you, my girl—do you think I'll let you be massacred just because most of our good-for-nothing species is due to be wiped out? Believe me, if there's going to be one man survive the slaughter, there'll be one woman too—just to start the new world right! Do you get me?"

As he crept nearer to her along the web, his little black eyes widened in a leer.

A quarter of an hour later, the full implications of his words became clear. Red-Hood and the other Saturnians had returned; and, ringing their captives about in a glittering circle, had demanded their decision. And Eleanor and Gates had defied them with a resolute "No!" regardless of the thunderous rumblings and the spouts of smoke that came from their masters' lips.

But Dunbar took another track.

"Worthy visitors from Saturn," he said, with mincing gestures, "I am glad to co-operate with you. But, in return, I ask one small boon."

"What boon?"

"If I help you, O noble ones, I must do so without restraint. But this cannot be unless you grant me the favor I ask. You see, O Lords, we Earth-men are so made that we cannot do our best work without a woman at our side. So I crave of you—spare the life of this female here; release her, so that she may labor with me."

A snort from Red-Hood drowned out Eleanor's shocked protests.

"But this woman, O Earthling, has refused to co-operate. She deserves the fate worse than death, which we have in store for her."

"Women, O Lords, are ever fickle and changeable of mind. If you will but spare her, I will see that she will co-operate."

The Saturnians held a brief conference among themselves, in tones like rapid gurglings. Then Red-Hood turned back toward Dunbar. "It is so, O Negneg! On our planet, too, the female of the species is fickle, and changes her mind like the lightning." And then, pointing scornfully at Gates. "Do you also ask us to spare your other companion?"

"Not so, O Lords. I ask the woman only…"

ELEANOR'S despairing cry was muffled amid the bellowing of the Saturnians, as they once more conferred, punctuating their debate with flashes of their many-colored armor, and with innumerable puffs of smoke, in a discussion that lasted for many minutes.

Finally, discharging sulphur fumes from little orifices at the ends of his long twining fingers, Red-Hood turned back to his Quisling.

"Let it be so!" he rattled out. "On one condition, we will release the woman. She will serve as a pledge for the faithful performance of your promise. If you fail us, by even the minutest fraction of a fraction of a degree, be sure she will not escape, but will perish along with you on the Barbs of Slow Agony!"

Eleanor gasped; and peering up into the relentless red eyes of her captors, knew that all protest would be futile.

"Zoltevi! Zoltevi! Quimboson!" she heard Red-Hood rasping, as one of his long tentacled arms motioned to two retainers. And after a brief interchange in their native tongue, the pair stepped forth, and she felt the octopus arms of one of the giants winding about her, while Dunbar was matched up in the claws of the second.

"My followers will give you your instructions!" Red-Hood growled at his new servant; while Eleanor, with swimming head, felt herself being borne down the great swaying web.

"Have faith! Have faith! We will win out yet!" she thought she heard a familiar voice calling after her. Or was it that, in her bewilderment, she had only imagined? For her last glimpse at Gates showed him standing erect and defiant enough, but so feeble-looking, of such midget size beside the many-armed, tailed monsters that towered above him to the height of the great dinosaurs of vanished ages!

CHAPTER FIVE
Paralyzed!

COMPARED with Gates as he stared up at his captors, Daniel in the lion's den may have considered himself almost among friends.

For a moment after the departure of the two other humans along with Zoltevi and Quimboson, no sound was audible except that of the threshing, sighing cables, and of the deep, throaty breathing of the monsters.

Then in silence—a silence more terrible than any spoken threat—Red-Hood advanced toward his victim. Gates, sensing his sinister intention, spontaneously pressed back. But Red-Hood drew nearer still, this time with a ten-foot stride. And Gates retreated to the extreme outer edge of the platform. Another inch, and he would have fallen!

But before he could plunge to a welcome deliverance, his persecutor's long tail shot out. With a rapid whirring motion, sounding a little like the warning buzz of a rattlesnake, it flicked by his left arm. And this time it did not miss. A glancing stroke touched him painlessly, leaving an abrasion hardly more noticeable than the prick of a pin.

But instantly something else occurred—something all too noticeable! Gates felt a numbness shoot along the arm, which took on the lifeless feeling of a jaw into which a dentist has pumped several charges of Novocain. And from the arm the feeling spread to his left shoulder, then over to the right shoulder, then down toward his abdomen, and up his neck, and along the right arm, and through both legs to the toes.

It all happened in a matter of seconds. Almost before he had had time to grasp the full dread facts, he found himself paralyzed. Yes, paralyzed practically completely! Except for a slight wriggling movement in his feet and fingers, he was unable to stir! In his horror, he attempted to cry out; but his tongue would not obey the impulse; all that came forth was a whisper-thin gurgling. Meanwhile, no longer able to maintain an upright position, he had sagged to the floor of the web, where he lay like a bundle of rags.

Strangely enough, however, the higher nerve centers appeared unaffected; his mind had not lost any of its clarity. It was, in fact, as though his mental reactions had suddenly been heightened, now that his physical frame was as if dead.

After a minute of silent gloating, during which he stood leering down at the victim, Red-Hood drew wide his green-gray lips, and huskily inquired.

"How do you feel now, O Earthling? That was what we call a tail-prick. Had the blow struck beneath the surface, you would have perished. But that would not have served our purpose. You can do more for us alive than dead."

SAVAGE and determined was the secret compact that Gates made with himself: he would perish in agony, a hundred times over, sooner than voluntarily help his captors by so much as the flick of one finger!

But Red-Hood, as if aware of his thoughts, twisted those great bag-like lips of his into a sardonic grin, and grumbled.

"It will not be up to you, my friend, whether you assist us or not. You see, there is nothing you can do against Lethemaz—the poison we apply with the tips of our tails. For a hundred thousand cycles our scientists have worked, until it has become the most efficient venom in the universe. A tenth of a drop—which is just what we used—will keep a mite like you paralyzed for days, unless we apply the proper antidote."

To Gates' horrified consciousness there had come the memory of certain wasps that injected a paralyzing fluid into their spider prey, keeping them alive but helpless for an indefinite period, so that they might nourish the next wasp generation.

But the fate of the spiders seemed almost enviable beside his own. For they at least would at last know an end to their captivity!

As this thought shot through his mind, he heard Red-Hood conferring in undertones with two subordinates. And the latter, after a moment, approached him and produced long cables, which they began to twist and loop about his body. For what purpose? He could not even guess. Yet the wicked twinkles in their three-cornered red eyes told him that they were up to some new villainy. A minute later, when they began to carry him down the web, amid the shimmering many-hued strands, how fervently he wished that he had seized his opportunity before it was too late and fallen off the platform to his doom!

TWELVE hours had gone by. The Crystal Planetoid, whirling on its orbit about the Earth, had swung back to the point at which the three humans had entered it. And a man and a girl, deposited by two invisible attendants, had found themselves back near the spot where their adventures had begun.

They had come down in a fog—which was not surprising, since fogs now hovered continually over the Earth; and their exact point of descent was an isolated spot in a city park, a mile or two from the laboratory. Dunbar recognized the place with a satisfied grunt, as he identified a certain rustic bridge over a small stream. "Good! Just ideal for a little chat…"

It seemed as if a huge shadow drifted over them and away, and vaguely they were aware that the two Saturnians had departed.

"What is there to chat about, Mr. Dunbar?" she flung back haughtily.

There was a silken purr in the man's voice. But determination marked his manner as he imposed himself in the girl's path.

"Now listen here, young lady. There are several things you might as well understand. The first is that you must cooperate."

"Cooperate?" she tossed back, shrilly, and paused long enough for a contemptuous fling of laughter. "Why who wouldn't die sooner than cooperate with those beasts— those dev—"

He had come closer to her, and his voice was coaxing, almost caressing.

"Do you think it was for their sake, Eleanor? Why do you think I saved you, except for your own precious self? If you will only cooperate with me—with *me*—"

"I'd rather cooperate with a viper…"

She had recoiled as though he was indeed the creature she had mentioned; and he found it necessary to seize her arm in order to prevent her departure.

"Come, let's forget all this, Eleanor. I know what nervous stress you are under. When you return to yourself, you will realize all that I have done for you. If I hadn't said a word in your behalf—"

"In *my* behalf! Good heavens, man!" she retorted, bitterly. "Don't you think I could have saved my own life if I had been willing to stoop to your kind of treason?"

"Treason or not, we shall see. We shall see. Meanwhile, I warn you, don't try to interfere when I fulfill my agreement—when I prepare those vats of compressed air—"

"And what if I report you to the authorities?"

"Report? You wouldn't be that stupid. You wouldn't drive me to action against you, would you?"

His tone had become subtly menacing as he leaned over her and whispered, almost furtively.

"Besides, have you not as much at stake as I, my girl? Remember, you are a pledge for my success. If I fail—"

"If you fail, I will give thanks to heaven."

With a determined effort, she had thrust herself forward; while he, following through the fog, pleaded and expostulated, in tones half like a lover, half like a taskmaster. At length, through the mist, there came a choked sobbing. And thin and faint, where two enormous creatures stood invisibly amid the vapors, there sounded an eerie squeak, like the muffled mockery of demons.

CHIEF OF POLICE JOE McCULLOUGH had settled back to a good fat cigar and the latest issue of the *Sports Digest*. His long legs stretched lankily across a chair; his heavy red face wore an expression almost of contentment, except when now and then he mopped the sweat from his brow with a crimson-bordered handkerchief. "Damn this heat," he finally muttered, glaring at the electric fan as if to accuse it of criminal conspiracy. And just then the door opened, and the sandy head of Sergeant Johannsen intruded.

"Sorry to butt in, Chief, but a dame out here wants to see you."

McCullough let out a low oath. "Didn't I tell you I don't want to be pestered? See her yourself, Johannsen. You're no slouch when it comes to dames." And, with a growl, he turned back to his issue of *Sports Digest*.

"But she swears she's gotta see you, Chief. Just can't do a thing with her. Something damned important, she says."

"Tell her to go to hell—"

Even as he spoke, a woman's face poked itself through the doorway. It was a face naturally comely, with clear blue eyes, and handsomely chiseled chin and brow; but just now she looked like the victim of a cyclone. Her clothes were rumpled; her disordered hair hung far down her forehead; there were tearstains beneath her eyes, which blazed with a wild, impatient light.

"Chief McCullough?" she demanded.

Had she been a man, she would have been ejected without debate. As it was, the Chief merely gaped at her, abashed, while awkwardly withdrawing his feet from their comfortable perch. "Yes, Ma'am. What can I do for you?"

"Something nobody else can do, Mr. McCullough. I know of a plot, sir—the most fiendish plot ever imagined. You'll hardly believe it, but I've just come down—well, down from one of the Crystal Planetoids, where they've hatched a scheme to capture the Earth."

McCULLOUGH gaped, and let the *Sports Digest* drop from his hands. He had had experience with crazy women before, but never with one who had dug out a scheme to capture the Earth. The best thing to do with her kind was to let them rave on. If you tried to interrupt them, they were apt to get hysterical.

And so it was with a polite but skeptical smile that he listened to her story of invaders as tall as a two-story house, who had enormous stinging tails and were invisible in ordinary light. Midway in her recital, he scowled reproof at Sergeant Johannsen, who seemed about to break out in open laughter; and, when she had finished, he thoughtfully took up his cigar, which he had put down for the moment, and remarked, with an attempt at courtesy.

"Well, now that's all too bad, Sister. The thing I'd advise you to do is to go home and sleep it off. These are queer times, you know. Why, with all this heat and tension, it's surprising we're not all seeing rattlesnakes and tigers. So you just have a good sleep, and tomorrow you'll feel better."

The girl stared at McCullough in dismay.

"But I'm not dreaming!" she insisted. "This is real—take my word for it, horribly real! There's a man—I can give you his name—who is working right now for the invaders, preparing tanks of compressed air. If you don't help—and immediately—"

She was interrupted by Johannsen, who, no longer able to contain himself, exploded in one mighty roar.

At the same time, she caught the amused glint in McCullough's eyes; and all at once she felt sick—sick to the very pit of her being. And, realizing the uselessness of further pleas, she turned without another word, and stumbled blindly toward the doorway.

CHAPTER SIX
An Offering from the Clouds

AT almost any other time in modern history, the disappearance of a promising young scientist would have created a sensation. As it was, the newspapers were so preoccupied with other events that they merely noted incidentally that "Ronald Gates, a technician employed by the Merlin Research Institute, has dropped mysteriously out of sight. No clue to his whereabouts has been found either at his lodgings or his place of employment. Suspicions of suicide, and of kidnapping for ransom, have not been confirmed."

Yet hardly was this story printed when extraordinary rumors began to be heard. So wild, so fantastic were the tales that most hearers shook their heads skeptically; newspapers denied them space; and even the most credulous old wives found belief stretched to the breaking point. But there were many who swore to the authenticity of the accounts. Ronald Gates, they attested, had been seen again; had been seen dangling in air, like a fly in a spider's web! About him were thin shimmering strands, which vanished into a mist; while he himself swung not many feet above the Earth, was both gagged and bound. Some declared that he was inert, and dead as a stone; but others averred that they had seen him making frantic movements with his feet, and with the tips of his fingers.

Among the few who listened seriously to these reports was Eleanor Firth. Rousing herself from the sick bed in which she had been confined for two days, suffering from what the doctor diagnosed as "nervous delusions," she set out toward the field at the outskirts of town, where, she had been told, the dangling apparition had been seen.

As she left the house, a skulking form slunk from behind a tree half a block away; and slithered to the nearest phone booth. She did not see the figure; but thought that it was by a queer coincidence that, after she had boarded a street car ten minutes later, she saw a taxicab just keeping pace with the trolley, and inside the vehicle recognized the slim dark shape of Dunbar.

At first she thought of turning back. But thinking that she might have made a mistake in identification, or that Dunbar might turn off in some other direction without seeing her, she continued on her way.

Twenty minutes later, when the car had reached its terminal, the taxicab was still a little behind.

But she could give little thought just then to the cab and its occupant. Through the mist she saw some vacant lots about a hundred yards away, where a crowd was assembled. And, with a fluttering heart, she pressed forward, racing rather than walking toward the crowd in the field.

AT the outskirts of the throng she joined the others in staring vaguely upward into the hazes, although at first she saw nothing.

"Why, he just seems to come and go," she heard a neighbor remarking. "Dips down, and then pops up again like a jack-in-the-box. You'd think he was held on strings."

"There he is!" a child cried out, eagerly. "Oh, Mamma, look! He's upside down!"

Surely enough, a figure was drifting out of the dense ceiling of fog. It was a figure as stiff and lifeless-looking as a manikin, except for the spasmodic twitching of the feet and fingers. And it was, as the child had exclaimed, upside down! Nothing could be weirder or more unnatural-looking than the way in which it slowly approached, in a diver's posture, with its arms outspread beneath it, and its feet uppermost. Obviously, it was supported by unseen hands or cables; yet Eleanor, no matter how she strained her eyes, could catch no glimpse of those cobweb strands which, she knew, encompassed it in a thick web.

For a moment or two, as she stared in a ghastly fascination, recognition did not come to her. Then all at once she cried out in astonished, dreadful certainty. That frank, open face, with the aquiline nose and broad, high forehead; those masses of coffee-brown hair, lying disheveled along the brow—how could she help recognize them, even though the tanned skin was covered with a dense stubble, and the once-mobile features looked inflexible as marble!

"Ronny! Ronny!" she exclaimed, sagging for support against a fat woman, who grumbled at her aberrations. And even as she spoke, she thought that she was answered by a glint in the eyes of the floating apparition. Yes, surely there was a responsive gleam! A vivid, deep fire which no paralysis could quench! She knew, she knew that Ronny had seen her, had recognized her!

But, at the same time, his eyes were kindled with such sorrow, such suffering that she thought of a martyr writhing at the stake.

Downward he floated, until he dangled but ten or twelve feet above her head. Only ten or twelve feet, she thought, yet what infinities between them. But almost immediately, he began to retreat. Jerked by the unseen cords, he slowly arose, was gradually pulled around to a horizontal position, and mounted until by degrees he was lost in the mist. And, all the while, from the watching crowd, came cries of wonder and amazement.

But just as the figure disappeared, Eleanor noticed something hardly less extraordinary. She could have sworn that, a moment before, a man had stood just to her right, had pressed almost elbow to elbow with her; and she knew that he had not strolled away. Yet suddenly she heard a groan from where he had been; then a swift swishing; and, turning, found that he was gone. Literally, he had vanished into thin air!

The next moment, when a frightened woman began crying, "John, John, where are you? For goodness' sake, where are you, John?" it seemed inevitable that there should be no response.

BUT her mind had no chance to dwell upon the incident. For she felt someone tapping her upon the shoulder; and, turning, stared into the dark, sardonically grinning face that she wished to see least of all faces on Earth.

How she hated him for the triumphant leer with which he devoured her! How she detested the manner in which he spoke, bowing urbanely, and with an ironic purr in his voice. "Ah, Eleanor...nice to meet you here." Somehow, she had the feeling of a bird in the hunter's hands.

"What a piece of good luck for us both, meeting like this," he murmured. "Better step over this way, Eleanor, there are some things to talk over."

"I can't imagine what," she denied.

But she caught the warning glint in his eyes. "Be unreasonable, young lady, and I don't answer for the consequences..."

In any case, she reflected, she could not stand here arguing with him; could not make a public spectacle of herself. And so, choking down the voice of inner warning, she followed him toward the waiting taxicab.

As they started off, a cry rang from the crowd; and, looking up, she saw the dangling figure emerging again from the mist. Strangely, it was propelled—almost thrust—in her direction, until it floated a mere half a dozen feet overhead. The face, as before, was rigid as rock, but the eyes glared with anger—anger fierce, vehement, concentrated, which seemed to focus in two fierce fire-points of light. Eleanor noticed how Dunbar, after a single glance, winced and turned away—slunk away, it seemed to her, in the manner of a whipped hound.

Upon reaching the taxicab, the girl hesitated. That warning voice, stronger now and more insistent, bade her not to enter. But the man's tones, soft and coaxing, appealed, "There's something I must tell you—I must, Eleanor, if you want to save yourself and our friend up above."

The plea for herself alone would not have sufficed; but at the reference to Ronald she felt herself yielding.

"Come, let's drive around town a while—anywhere at all you say," he suggested, "before having you taken back home."

After all, she thought, what harm in driving around a bit? She was almost exhausted, and it would be so much easier not to have to go home by trolley! Besides, she was so faint that there was little power in her to resist Dunbar's will.

And so she found herself preceding him into the cab, although still that warning voice cautioned, "Don't! Don't! Don't!"

"Anywhere around the suburbs," Dunbar instructed the driver. And then the door slammed, and they were on their way. But, as the wheels whirred beneath her, she would have given her last penny to be safely on the ground again.

Subtly, insidiously, her companion's manner had changed. There was a menacing note beneath the silken purr as he turned to her, and demanded, "And now, young lady, maybe you will tell me why you have not been cooperating?"

SHE writhed; withdrew from him as far as possible; and made no answer. How idiotic of her to have let him lure her into the taxi.

"Maybe you will tell me," he went on, "why it was you went to the police to report me? No! Don't say you didn't. I have informants…"

"That is to say, you've been shadowing me with spies, Mr. Dunbar?" she retorted, turning upon him with spirit.

"I don't care a damn what you call it," he snarled. "Simple fact is I couldn't afford to take any chances. But I really didn't think you'd be imbecilic enough to report me—since we're both in the same boat. If the Saturnians murder me, they murder you too. Remember that…"

"So that's what you decoyed me into the car to say, Mr. Dunbar?"

"I didn't decoy you. But I did want to warn you. If you give me your solemn promise, Eleanor, to keep a tight lock on your tongue, and not interfere with me any further, I'll let you go about your way. But not unless!"

"I don't propose to argue with you, Mr. Dunbar." Her tones were slow, incisive, cutting. "Now if you'll have the kindness to give the driver my address—"

"Not so fast there, my girl. We've still got some things to thresh out. Just because you don't seem to care about your own life, it doesn't follow I'm going to let you throw mine away."

At last the mask was falling off. He glared; his teeth bit into his lower lip; his manner was truculent. "Good Lord, Eleanor, don't you know those Saturnians are watching everything you do? How long do you think their patience will last? What do you suppose old Red-Hood will do when he finds you're all set to betray him?"

"Betray *him?*" Scornfully she laughed. "So that's the only betrayal you're thinking of? Now will you kindly give that driver my address?"

He made no move to obey.

"If you won't, then I will !" she decided, starting up.

But a powerful hand had seized her, and thrust her back, "I tell you, my girl, we've got to thresh this out!"

"I tell you, there's nothing to thresh out!"

Before her inner vision there flashed again a figure, with pain-tormented eyes, who dangled helplessly high in air. And she clenched her fists, and secretly swore a bitter oath.

"So then it's not peace, but a sword?" he flung out, as if reading her thoughts. "In that case, you force me to act in self-defense…"

Despite the quietness of his manner, she was becoming more and more frightened. His heart fluttered; she remembered again that voice of warning, which she had not heeded; and felt suddenly too weak and helpless to make the attempt—the obviously futile attempt to call out to the driver.

From an inner pocket he had pulled a little vial filled with a dark-brown fluid. And, from another pocket, he drew a hypodermic needle.

"Lucky for us both that, being a chemist, I can prepare my own formulas," he went on, with an oily drawl. "Now this won't do you any real harm, Eleanor, so I'd advise you not to struggle. That will only make it harder for you, and not help at all in the end."

"For God's sake," she screamed, "what are you going to do?"

Wildly she stared out of the taxicab, with some vague idea of yelling for help or jumping. But they were speeding along an almost houseless suburban road, with not a person in sight; and to attempt to jump, even if she should succeed, would be mere suicide.

Meanwhile he had dipped the needle in the brown fluid, and she saw its thin, sinister point approaching.

"Just hold out your arm," he advised. "It will be all over in a second."

She was to remember hazily that she attempted a shriek, which was muffled by his throttling hand. She was to remember that she struggled spasmodically; beat at her oppressor with blind, self-protective fury. But this was all that she did recollect, aside from the fact that there came a sharp stabbing sensation just above her wrist...followed by a shooting pain in her head, an overwhelming dizziness, a reeling and swaying, and, suddenly and mercifully, a black, dreamless unconsciousness.

CHAPTER SEVEN
Prisoners' Progress

LETHEMAZ, the paralyzing drug of the Saturnians, had one quality for which Gates was sometimes thankful, and which sometimes he bitterly cursed. Despite the total incapacity of his body, his brain, as we have seen, was able to work with new keenness and clarity. Yet his increased mental awareness only added to his agony. For it made him see the horror, the helplessness of his plight in even more pitiful sharpness.

Eleanor had been right in supposing that his eyes had glowed with recognition as he dangled in air above her. She had been right in believing that he had glared at the sight of Dunbar. But she could not have known what torment seethed behind that rigid brow of his. She could not have known the tantalizing madness of one who, hour after hour, realizes that he is being used as a tool for the furies of destruction, yet is powerless to speak or act. Nor could she have guessed what dire new discoveries the captive had made.

From time to time Gates was carried back to the Crystal Planetoid, where a sting from one of the monsters' tails applied a deparalyzing fluid. Thus he found occasional relief—which, however, was not to be credited to any feeling of mercy on the part of the captors. No...for he could not be fed while paralyzed. And thanks to the way in which he was jolted around, he had to be given food every few days if he was not to perish.

As yet, it was not only the purpose of the invaders to keep him alive, but to obtain as many living humans as possible. Dozens of men and women, as he saw to his dismay, had been brought to the Planetoid and paralyzed. Like flies tangled in the webs of gigantic spiders, the victims lay scattered about the webs. And Gates realized that he was, in a sense, responsible. Yes, he had been the unwilling tool to trap them; it was as a bait that he had been dangled above the Earth…so that, when the people congregated beneath, the Saturnians might take their pick and whisk the victims away while the crowd was too preoccupied to be aware what had happened.

But why did they desire so many humans? Gates had the boldness to put this question to Red-Hood during one of his de-paralyzed intervals; and, to his surprise, the monster immediately rasped out an answer:

"Negneg, surely you have not the brains of a gnat, else you would have guessed! We capture you Earthlings so as to dangle you above the Earth as a lure to capture other Earthlings!"

"And why capture other Earthlings?"

"Why?" The giant's red eyes twinkled with amusement, as at a child who persists in asking the ridiculous. "Naturally, we want specimens of all the human fauna, of every race and color, so that we may skin and dry them in the interest of science, and bring them back to Saturn as specimens for the Museum of Unnatural History."

Noting the horror with which Gates greeted this explanation, Red-Hood went on to state.

"After all, Negneg you should be grateful to us for seeking to preserve some trace of your species, instead of obliterating it entirely. You Earth creatures have no sense of gratitude…"

Thanks to this information, Gates' mind was more busy than ever with the problem of circumventing the Saturnians. His first thought was to destroy his own value to them by means of a hunger strike. But the result was that his food, in liquid form, was forced down his throat; while the Saturnians, apparently fearing that he would resort to other means to take his own life, vigilantly followed his every movement.

Nevertheless, after a time, an idea did come to him—an idea that at first appeared wild and impossible, and yet seemed to offer the only prospect, however remote, of regaining his freedom.

BUT before he could try out the scheme, matters on Earth went from bad to worse.*

To say that the world was frantic would be to understate. Who of us that lived through those cataclysmic days will ever forget how men walked the streets with white, harried faces, their beards untended, their clothes in soiled disarray? Who will ever forget the sense of being at a world's end? Who will not shudder again as he recalls the appeals made to scientists by government officials—the desperate appeals headlined in the papers and blared through the radio: "As you value your lives, find the cause of the disturbance! Find the cause of this monstrous distortion of nature! Give us a remedy! Give us a remedy soon, soon—or it will be too late!"

But scientists labored hard and long—labored fifteen or eighteen hours a day, and found no remedy. Some, in fact, maintained that no remedy was possible. Who that is now of middle age cannot re-live the day when Dr. Arnold Woodrum, of the Cyclops Observatory, let it be known in an interview that he believed the Solar System to be passing through a region of space crossed by radio-active forces, which would gradually raise the temperature until all

---

*Daily the unexplained thickening of the atmosphere was growing more noticeable. Daily the air was becoming heavier, more sluggish, more humid, and hotter. Thunder storms of greater violence than ever had become of daily occurrence in widely scattered sections of the Earth. Droughts in some regions, and floods in others, had scarred the surface of the planet. Temperatures running well into the low hundreds were now common in districts where eighty had been considered hot. Some sections, indeed, had become uninhabitable.

By the first of August, the deaths ascribed to the heat in the great cities of the eastern United States had risen to a daily average of scores of thousands. Mass migrations were in progress from tropical and sub-tropical regions— by every obtainable device, by liner, freighter and tugboat, by private car, truck and airplane, the inhabitants of South and Central America were streaming toward the temperate and polar regions. In India, scores of millions were flocking into the Himalayas; in Africa, the population was perishing like ants, and no count of the mortality was even attempted; in the South Seas the customary trade winds did not blow, and the waters became too warm for bathing. For the first time in history the Antarctic Continent, its glaciers beginning to melt, offered promise of becoming habitable; while men of daring laid plans to establish winter homes in Labrador and Greenland. Meanwhile vast once-verdant sections of America, Asia and Europe had been seared to a leafless brown. —Ed.

life was burned to a crisp? In the absence of any more definite knowledge, this view was widely accepted. And prayers and lamentations became universal.

It is a never-to-be-forgiven crime that the one man who, in these circumstances, could have poured out valuable information, was a man who kept his lips tight-shut.

IN A private laboratory improvised in his apartment, Philip Dunbar was hard at work. Motors buzzed about him; tubes and wires were woven intricately across the room: while dark hissing vapors and spouts of steam issued from numerous valves and retorts. Piled deep in one corner, were dozens of great torpedo-shaped steel tubes, some of them sealed, some of them ending in complicated coils of rubber tubing; and it was to these that the worker gave his chief attention.

After several hours, Dunbar paused; sighed; mopped his sweaty brow; turned a switch that sent the motors groaning to a halt; and, after unlocking the door, stepped into an adjoining room.

There he was confronted by a girl who, her hands joined behind her back and her teeth biting into her lower lip, had been pacing slowly back and forth.

She cast him a scornful glance, and continued ranging the floor.

"Listen, Eleanor," he said. "You don't have to carryon like this. Don't act like a prisoner. Make yourself at home. In that case in the foyer, you'll find some mighty interesting books—"

There was fury in her manner as she turned upon him. "Well, what am I but a prisoner? Do you want me to bow down and thank you for keeping me locked here these last seven days?"

His tone was quiet, restrained, almost reproachful.

"But what do you expect, Eleanor? Surely, you understand the circumstances—"

Her blue eyes blazed. He had never before noticed how strong was the curve of her chin, how firm the set of her jaw. "Circumstances?" she derided. "All that I understand is that you drugged me—kidnapped me—brought me here forcibly, with the help of that hireling of yours, the taxi driver—"

"I've heard all about that before," he broke in, still without losing control of himself. "I know I've behaved rudely, Eleanor. But, after all, why not give me credit for some things? Haven't I treated you decently here? Have I so much as touched you with one finger, even though all the while I've been burning with love?"

She shuddered, and recoiled.

"Why do you act as if I were dirt beneath your feet?" he rushed on. "Haven't I done everything to make you comfortable? Haven't I fed you properly? Good heavens, Eleanor, don't you know that I love you…?"

He had pressed toward her, his eyes hot and desirous, while she had backed into the remotest corner of the room.

"And you expect *me* to love a traitor?" she shot at him. "Am I to sit by and adore you for playing Quisling to the whole Earth?"

"That isn't fair, Eleanor," he protested. "Why, most girls would feel indebted to me for life for saving them. You will too…someday. You're just a little hysterical now, that's the trouble. But come, come, a little kiss is what you need to soothe you…"

SHE saw the black-moustached face drawing closer. She saw the black eyes sparkling with predatory glee. She knew that in an instant the long twining fingers would be feeling their way about her. And she realized the futility, the folly of calling out for help. Nevertheless, a scream was upon her lips.

Then, when already she could feel his breath, hot and fetid as that of some beast of prey, relief came from an unexpected quarter.

A sharp sudden rattling and snapping sounded from the direction of the laboratory. And through the open door she could see how, miraculously, the laboratory window flew open as if in a violent gale, although not the slightest breeze was blowing.

Dunbar, hearing the noise, wheeled about, and gasped.

"By Christopher, how'd that happen?"

Then solemnly, after a moment, he added, "Why, I could swear I locked that window this morning..."

As if in answer, several thick steel rods on the laboratory table began to dance back and forth like dry leaves in the wind.

"Holy Jerusalem..." he half-whispered, backing away. "Am I going crazy?"

"No, negneg, you are no crazier than ever!" returned a rasping voice, seemingly from nowhere. "But we have been paying you a visit of inspection."

The two human hearers stood with wide-open mouths, speechless.

"I am Quimboson, the servant of the Peerless Red One," went on the invisible. "I am perched outside your window now, on a web you cannot see. Finding the window closed, I pulled it open. One of my hands is in the room, shuffling these little objects on the table. I can reach in wherever I wish. Shall I prove it?"

Feeling the sudden pressure of a clammy paw against his brow, Dunbar was quite convinced.

Now all at once the tone of the invisible became harsher, more menacing.

"Earthling," he growled, "I am much displeased! The tail of the Peerless Red One will lash out in wrath when he hears my report. For instead of attending to your duties, we find you in dalliance with the female of your species."

"But only for a moment!" pleaded Dunbar, in a cowed manner.

"A moment too much. I always thought it was a mistake to spare the female. When I tell the Peerless Red One, he will order her to be stung to death. Stung to death instantly! So I shall recommend, O Earthling, and the Peerless Red One always takes my advice on these minor matters…"

Eleanor's gasp of horror was drowned out by Dunbar's appeal.

"But you've got to spare her, O Quimboson! Otherwise, how can I do my best work? On my oath, I shall waste no more time with her—"

"Your oath, O Earthling, is as a sword of sand. But no more of this empty talk. I go now—I go!"

There came a whirring and a screeching, sounding oddly like mocking laughter; then the laboratory window banged to a close, and all became silent.

IT was several minutes before Eleanor, her face white, turned to Dunbar. "For God's sake, don't you see—don't you see, you *must* let me go! They'll be back here—they'll be back soon, and strike me dead—"

But Dunbar had returned to the laboratory, where he had switched on the motors.

"If I do let you go, they'll strike me dead," he snapped back. "Lord! Haven't you gotten me into trouble enough already?"

So speaking, he slammed the door with a violent jerk.

Eleanor, sinking into a chair, her head buried in her hands, was driven more sharply than ever against the same dreary problem that had baffled her during all these days of captivity. How to escape? The single door to the apartment was securely barred. The single accessible window gave upon a concrete court four stories beneath—and, lest she be tempted to leap out, her approach was impeded by a barbed wire barricade. Telephone connections had been cut—and there was no neighbor to whom she could call through the sound-proof walls. No...she was utterly balked!

Still, what matter that she might die a little ahead of the mass of mankind? After all, that was of no importance—but what might be vital was her chance to warn others of Dunbar's crime against humanity, if only she could escape! True, she had already tried to give warning, and had merely been laughed at; yet she had lately conceived a new idea that might offer a dim hope if once she were free.

Half swooning with the heat, she heard through the laboratory door the whirring of motors; and her head ached dully, and she burst into tears, for the dead have as much chance of rising as she had of beating down the monstrous forces ranged against her.

CHAPTER EIGHT
The Revolt of Yellow-Claws

HOUR after hour Gates had been watching his captors. Hour after hour he had been scheming, observing, hoping. With the heightened mental quickness of his paralyzed state, he was searching for a weak spot in the armor of the foe. "Surely," he reflected, "there must be some flaw that makes them vulnerable." And it was this thought that put him on the track of the wild idea that appeared to offer his only prospect of freedom.

By carefully following everything the invaders said and did, he was able to grasp the meaning of many words and phrases in their language. Even with his remarkable new rapidity of apprehension, he learned no more than a four-year-old might learn of English—yet this little went far, particularly as the enemy did not suspect that any mere Earthling could be so intelligent.

But it was his eyes and not his ears that enabled him to fathom the secret of the Saturnians' greatest power: their ability to make themselves invisible. Whenever one of the monsters wished to vanish from sight, he merely dusted himself with a pale-blue powder from a purple-veined container. Evidently the powder—acting somewhat like a catalyzing agent of some sort—had the effect of causing the rays of light to pass completely through any object, thereby rendering it invisible. But did it make things invisible also to Saturnian eyes? The answer was in the affirmative: a Saturnian dusted with Amvol-Amvol could not be seen by any of his fellows, nor could the webs and cables, when concealed beneath this substance, be observed by their makers.

This was, however, of little importance to Red-Hood and his followers; for they relied upon sight much less than did human beings. They were guided largely by what they called the Communication Sense: certain vibrations in the air, set up by their tails, were recorded by a bulging organ just under the left ear of each of the creatures; and thus they were able to learn of their whereabouts and doings of their kindred even when they could not be seen.

So, at least, Gates concluded after long and careful observation. And his scheme for escape was built upon this knowledge.

BUT for a long while the plan did not take definite shape. And meanwhile he came to realize more keenly than ever how dangerous it would be to provoke his masters needlessly.

For they had surpassingly quick and violent tempers; their rage was, literally, like a tornado. Many a time Gates, lying helpless in paralysis on a web in the Planetoid, was the terrified witness to one of their disputes. He was seldom able to decide just what the quarrel was about, the first that he ever knew of it was when a blast like a siren ripped at his eardrums. Then other siren blasts would follow; then spouts of smoke would leap through the air, and the acridness of sulphur would torment his nostrils; then, if he were in a favored position, he would see the adversaries facing one another, their tails lashing the atmosphere in long loops and spirals, their octopus arms threshing and writhing, while the screeching and bellowing would rise to a crescendo as of battling fiends, and the eyes of the competitors would blaze with fiery red flashes.

There was one fight, in particular, which Gates would never forget. As usual, he had at first no idea of the cause; but the tumult this time was more diabolical than ever before. Paralyzed, he hung on a web several hundred feet above the floor of the Planetoid, in a grandstand position to view the affray. Among the lower meshes and cables, directly beneath him, Red-Hood stood amid steamy clouds of gas. And opposite him was an almost equally huge Saturnian, whose distinguishing features, as Gates saw it, was the clay-yellow coloration of his long tentacle-like claws.

For a tense minute the two creatures stood opposite one another, like bulls ready to charge. Then out shot Red-Hood's tail, striking with a crash against the rainbowed armor of the foe. And Yellow-Claws' breast was streaked with a golden-yellow spurt of blood; and crimson fires shot from his lips in curling tongues. Wrathfully his own tail lashed out, but missed his antagonist, who had leapt back with hair-trigger agility; while from Red-Hood's throat came such a howl that the very web trembled.

Gates was aware that a score of Saturnians stood watching intently below, at a safe distance, like spectators about a prize ring. He heard them whirring with excitement as the two opponents fended for positions. Then, to his astonishment, he saw Red-Hood springing forward, his octopus arms outspread, like some monster of a nightmare. Yellow-Claws was ready for the onslaught; and for a moment the two furies clashed, wrestling with hurricane vehemence…so that they seemed little more than a gigantic whirl of squirming, rotating, threshing arms, legs and tails.

But soon, with an unearthly cry, one of the creatures detached himself, and with cyclonic speed darted up the web. So swiftly did he travel that at first Gates was unable to determine that it was Yellow-Claws that fled, while Red-Hood pursued close behind. Up and down and sideways along the web, with all manner of athletic twists and wrigglings, the embattled pair rushed, now scores of feet above the observer, now; hundreds of feet beneath. Once Yellow-Claws lost his grip and fell, but, with gymnastic swiftness, clutched at a dangling cable, and saved himself barely in time. Once, slashed in the neck by Red-Hood's tail, he let out such a roar that Gates thought he had been slain. Once it was Red-Hood who, torn by his opponent's tail, yelled in agony. Several times the rivals were screened from one another amid smoke clouds.

Yet it was but a few minutes before the fight was over. Yellow-Claws, one of his arms almost half severed, waved his tail high in air, and uttered a shrill, "Wikyi! Wikyi! Wikyi!" (I give up! I give up!") And Red-Hood, with a contemptuous snort, lashed out at him for a final time; and then, acknowledging the conclusion of peace, screamed triumphantly, and majestically stalked away.

BUT for hours the defeated giant sat on a web just below Gates, tending his wounds. His armor had lost its iridescence; thick smears of golden-orange covered its gashed surface. Yet Yellow-Claws' three-cornered eyes blazed with unsubdued anger; and his greenish-gray lips were twisted into grimaces of hate. Vengefully he muttered to himself, ignoring the presence of an Earthling in the web above; vengefully he muttered three words, "Zugavl! Zugavl! Zug!"

Gates did not need to know the meaning of these expressions; from the manner in which they were uttered, he was sure that they boded no good for the Peerless Red One.

At about the same time, he made another important observation. Fighting was not the only bad habit of the Saturnians; they were subject to a far worse vice—that of inhaling Kishkash. This word, which was constantly on the monsters' lips, referred to the fumes from the burning of a certain dried leaf from Saturn. Nothing like it had ever been known on Earth; a single whiff was enough to give Gates nausea; it had the foulest odor that had ever attacked his nostrils, being like the concentrated stench of putrefaction.

Yet to the Saturnians it was ambrosia. They never tired of sitting over little pots of the glowing substance, greedily drawing the smoke into their lungs, amid sighs and grunts of satisfaction. And the effect upon them was, to say the least, peculiar: after a time, they would fall into a stupor, and would lie on their backs on the floor, kicking their legs and lashing out with their arms and tails, evidently unable to control their own movements. Some of them, in fact, spent half their time in this state of delicious drunkenness.

It was from this fact that Gates hoped to profit. Eagerly he watched for his opportunity; and one day, when he was fortunately in a deparalyzed state, the chance arrived. It had been a time of celebration, in commemoration of a Saturnian holiday, honoring the great hero Dupepu, who, it seems, had wiped out seventeen nations; and Kishkash, which was considered indispensable on all festal occasions, had been burned with exceptional lavishness. As a result, every visible Saturnian lay on the floor of the Planetoid, kicking up his heels, while whirring and mumbling the delicious nonsense of intoxication.

Here, Gates instantly realized, was a heaven-sent opportunity. Left unguarded for the first time, he crawled down from the swinging platform where he had been placed for safekeeping; and, risking his life on a long rope-ladder, made his way to a portion of the web featured by several round dangling purple pouches. In these bags, he had observed, the natives kept their Amvol-Amvol, the powder of invisibility. Once he had obtained this, his scheme would be already half consummated!

And what was to keep him from the Amvol-Amvol? Could he believe his senses?—believe that the precious substance was unwatched and free for the taking? Yes! This seemed actually to be the case. Barring the remote possibility that one of the Saturnians would revive in time to interfere, there was nothing between him and his goal!

SO down and down he climbed, along the interwoven meshes of swaying, shimmering cables; down like a seaman descending the riggings of a vessel. At length he had reached the pouches. The nearest of them, as large as a watermelon, was within arm's grasp. The top, moreover, was wide open! And, inside, he could see the sky-blue powder that for days he had dreamt of obtaining!

Yet for just a second he hesitated. He could not guess what it was that chilled his hand; that restrained for a moment his desire for the magical substance. Was it some voice of hidden warning? He could not say. He only knew that he laughed silently at himself; then, with reviving eagerness, shot his hand into the pale-blue dust.

The substance was downy soft to the touch, yet was cold as stone, and caused a tingling, faintly stinging sensation to creep along his skin. Hungrily his fingers closed over it; then, with a good handful in their clutch, began to withdraw.

But, as they did so, Gates was startled by a sudden grating noise, followed by a sharp click. And a violent pain shot through his wrist. Teeth of steel dug into his flesh; and, in horrible realization, he knew that he was caught!

Yes, caught like a wild beast snared in a wolf-trap! It is hard to say whether, in that first stunned instant, his pain or his alarm was the greater. Yet his mind at once took in the full dread import. The pouch was but a ruse; it was equipped with hidden jaws, which would close at the faintest touch, seizing the unwary intruder. Oh, why had he not had the brains to beware?

From the first, he saw that escape would be impossible. Those cruel jaws were so made that the more he struggled, the more tightly his arm would be wedged between them, and the more intense his agony—if he were not careful, his other wrist would be caught too! Knowing that he would be fettered here until his masters revived from their intoxication; and knowing also the terrible tempers of the tribe, he concluded that he would be better off dead.

It was as this thought bored at his brain that he heard a sound to his left. Low, stealthy, secretive, it yet had a vaguely familiar whirr. "Earthling, listen to me!"

His heart gave a convulsive leap. He felt that his last moment had come. So he had not been alone after all, had not been unguarded! One of his captors, garbed in invisibility, had been watching him, following his every movement, gloating in his helplessness as a cat gloats in the sufferings of a mouse!

"Earthling, listen to me!"

The words had been repeated, in the same stealthy manner.

"Who are you?" the prisoner found courage to gasp.

"Soon I shall say. First, let me free you from your misery."

THERE came a snapping sound; the steel jaws clattered apart; and Gates, to his astonishment, withdrew a bruised and bleeding wrist.

"The lower animals should not meddle with tools they do not understand," mumbled the unseen. "By my home-world's outer ring! You did not pull down the safety clasp before sticking in your hand!"

"But who—who are you?" repeated the captive, becoming bolder, although he could not believe that he had been freed for any good purpose.

"Who am I?" The speaker paused long enough for a burst of low whirring laughter. "I am Misthrumb, though that means nothing to you. I am he who fought yesterday with the Peerless Red One, and was driven off, may the curse of the Nine Planets fall on his foul bosom!"

"Oh—you mean, Yellow-Claws?"

"Yellow-Claws? Well, you may call me that, for my hands are of the soil yellow of royalty! My blood too is yellow, golden-yellow. I am as high-born as the Peerless Red One. Was I not designated by the Grand Potentate, the Barbelcoppi, to share the leadership of this expedition? And has the Peerless One not denied me at every turn— yes, may the demons of every vile disease prey upon him!"

Not knowing what to reply, Gates said nothing. But hope, dead only a minute before, had revived within him.

"As if he had not already injured me enough," went on the invisible one, "he ordered me to keep away from the great festival of Dupepu, whereat all my brothers make merry. Forbidden me to enjoy the delectable, sacred fumes of Kishkash! For that he shall suffer!" Yellow-Claws' tones, rasping and angry, indicated that the feud between the giants was far deeper than Gates has suspected. "And when I saw you creeping toward the Amvol-Amvol, O negneg, I knew that you would be the tool of my vengeance…"

"Me?" groaned the victim. Had he escaped the frying pan only to be plunged into the fire?

"Have no fear, Earthling. My purpose matches your own. To be sure, there are perils—appalling perils! Not to master them is to die a horrible death. But to prevail is to escape from the Peerless Red One—and to repay him in full measure for his crimes against us both. Are you ready to take the risk, O Earthling?"

"I am ready!"

"By the stars! That is more than I would have expected of one of your species. Then let us begin! We have but a little time before my brothers recover from the Kishkash."

Gates could not see the creature's yellow claws as they entered the pouch and drew out a pale blue powder. But he felt something soft, cool and tingling being sprinkled over his hands, his face, up his sleeves, and down his neck. And he had one of the strangest sensations of his life; for his body, even as he gazed at it, faded into a haze, and vanished. He could look through himself! He could see the meshwork of shimmering cables as if there was nothing between!

"Come…" whispered his projector. "There is no time to lose." And then angrily, beneath his breath, "Zugavl! Zugavl! Zug!"

Upheld and guided by Yellow-Claws—since his arms and legs, now that he could not see them, seemed oddly unreliable—Gates started once more down the web, above the spot where the intoxicated monsters, like huge over-turned beetles, lay on their backs with furiously wriggling tentacles, legs and tails.

CHAPTER NINE
Through the Barred Door

IF only she could get word to someone outside. If only someone could learn of her plight, she might be saved—and she might save the world! Such was the thought that kept pounding at Eleanor's brain as she sat stooped in her prison room, her head buried in her hands, while through the closed door came the buzzing and droning of motors.

Then by degrees an idea thrust itself upon her. As she moped alone in her dismal monotony, she had heard every evening the shuffling of someone ascending the steps just beyond the barred apartment door. The sound always came at the same time—at five minutes before six—and she could recognize the peculiar dreary noise as it approached. Might not the passer-by, whoever he was, become her rescuer? At first she thought of calling out to him; but realized that, even if he took heed, this would merely be to warn Dunbar, who would find ways to balk her plan.

No! She must communicate without being heard. But how? As if anticipating this very possibility, Dunbar had denied her all writing materials. She considered, indeed, the ancient device of a message written in her own blood, which she might scrawl on a fly-leaf torn from a book; but she feared that some chance blood-stain would furnish her captor with a fatal clue.

The thought of the books, however, gave her another idea. Leaping up with sudden alacrity, she went to the case Dunbar had mentioned, and eagerly selected a volume.

Passing through the room half an hour later; her oppressor paused with a grim smile to see her bent above "The Greycourt Murder Mystery."

"Ah!" he exclaimed, as he leaned over her shoulder for a glance at the title. "Didn't know you went in for that sort of stuff. Good idea, though. Takes your mind off your troubles. Literature of escape they call it."

He did not notice the ironic glint in her eyes, nor the faint quivering of her voice as she replied.

"Yes, that's it—literature of escape."

Had his mind not been preoccupied, he would have seen how her hands fluttered, and how tremulously she averted his gaze.

"Oh, by the way, might just as well tell you," he confided. "I've been making fine progress. In another five days if all goes well, I'll be able to set you free."

"Free?" she gasped, unbelievingly.

"Yes, I'll be done with my job by then—have all the compressed air tanks ready, in just another five days."

She started up as if she had been struck, allowing the book to slip to the floor unnoticed.

"Five days?" she repeated, blankly, realizing how little time remained for her to work in. "Five days…"

"Good lord but I'm getting fed up, slaving in this damnable heat," he muttered; and then, passing out of the room, threw out at her, with a burst of sardonic laughter, "Now, my girl, better get back to your—your literature of escape…"

Stunned, she reached for the book. Yet it was with fresh alertness, with a swift new eagerness, that she began racing through the pages. Only a few minutes later, she came to a passage that made her sit up with a start. Then hastily she reached for the little blue handbag she had carried at the time of her capture by Dunbar; and drew out a pair of nail scissors. Her eyes had a furtive look as she stared toward the doorway where Dunbar had disappeared; but her fingers worked swiftly and nimbly as they clipped away at the printed page.

SEVERAL hours later, Emanuel Knapp, a civil service employee, was on his way home to his top-floor apartment. As usual, he puffed and wheezed as he climbed the weary five flights in the old-fashioned "walk-up" building; and, as usual for many weeks past, he sweated in the deadly heat. Arriving at the fourth floor, he paused to regain his breath; and, as he did so, he became conscious of a low rustling, and saw a thin bit of paper being ejected beneath the door of Apartment 4E.

"Well now, isn't that funny," he thought; and, though not naturally a curious man, reached automatically for the paper.

As he opened it, he saw to his surprise that it was part of the title page of a book, and his eyes fell upon the conspicuous printed word, MURDER.

"What the heck! Am I going crazy with the heat?" he mumbled to himself; and noticing several smaller specks of paper fluttering loose from the larger one, he reached down for them also.

"For heaven's sake, rescue me!" he read on the first of the slips, which was printed in large book type; while another slip bore, in the same type, an even more startling notation, "I'm caught in the toils of the slimiest devil God ever put on Earth…"

Now Emanuel Knapp was not a man naturally quick of apprehension. Hence he was not certain that anything was really seriously amiss. "Most likely there's some crazy loon inside—or else it's just a practical joke," he reflected, as he scowled at the door of 4E.

Having thus solved the mystery, he wiped his streaming red brow, and bleakly started up the final flights of stairs.

But, as he did so, he spied a third printed slip at the base of the steps. And wearily he reached down for it.

"Lord help us, sir, don't hesitate a minute!" he read, "Not one minute, or it will be too late!"

"By gum," he meditated, "wonder if there mightn't be something in it after all. Maybe I ought to notify the police. No harm, anyway, in letting 'em know."

But the thought of retreating down those four long flights of stairs was far from inviting. However, his interest being aroused, he pressed one ear against the door of 4E. And, from within, he heard a low droning sound.

"By glory," he concluded, starting down the stairs, "maybe someone needs help, or maybe it's a counterfeiting gang…"

Fifteen minutes later, two officers of the law had marched in Knapp's company to the door of 4E. And after prolonged rapping and violent bell-ringing, the door had opened, to reveal a man in a chemist's stained white robe, who greeted them blandly, and professed great surprise at their call.

"Looks like you've got the wrong apartment, Officers," he protested, suavely, when shown the clippings picked up by Knapp. "I've been busy all day with some experiments in the laboratory. There's no one else in the place."

"Well, damn it, the story did look phoney to me!" admitted Officer O'Madden, glaring reproachfully at

Knapp. "What the hell…a regular cock-and-bull yarn! If the Chief hadn't ordered us to come…"

BUT Officer Frye was of a different state of mind. "Perfectly sure you're the only person here, Mister?" he demanded of Dunbar.

"Hasn't been another soul around for weeks."

"Sure of that?"

"Absolutely."

"Then what is that blue handbag doing over there on the settee?"

Dunbar could not quite control a startled gasp. His eyes flashed, and his lips twitched oddly. But he did not reply.

"Mind if I look at it?"

Dunbar, imposing himself in the way, started to protest. But the officer had already shoved himself into the room. In an instant he had snatched up the handbag and slipped open the clasp. And from within he had taken a small printed card, and read, "Miss Eleanor Firth."

"Firth? Eleanor Firth?" gasped O'Madden. "By crimps! Ain't that the girl what disappeared the other day? Why, her folks made one hell of a row about it. I was in the station when they came in. Foul play they suspected…"

A long weighted silence followed. Dunbar glanced furtively toward the door, as if looking for some easy way of escape. His eyes twinkled with the fury of a trapped animal.

"Well, maybe it's just what you call a coincidence," drawled Officer Frye. "Anyway, guess we'd better take a look around."

Despite Dunbar's protestations, the officers proceeded to essentially ransack the room—though without results.

And while they were peering under tables, behind sofas and into closets, Knapp stood with his nose pressed suspiciously against a locked door.

"Say, Officer, there's a funny smell coming from over here," he reported.

"The whole place smells funny, if you ask me," mumbled Frye. And then, turning to Dunbar, "Guess you'd better let us peep in there, mister,"

The chemist stood with his back firmly pressed against the door. "I'll be damned if I will! That's my private laboratory. I'm in the midst of an experiment, which will be ruined if I let any light in…"

"To hell with your experiment! Stand aside, mister!"

But not until two pairs of strong arms had flung him away did Dunbar forsake the door. And not until two strong pairs of shoulders had pressed themselves against the partition did the lock show signs of yielding. It was just when it began to crack that Dunbar made his dash toward the front entrance—to be thwarted by the lucky chance that Knapp blocked his way, giving Frye time to lay hands upon him, while O'Madden finished the little business of breaking down the door

As the barrier gave way, an unpleasant odor, a little like ether, penetrated to the men's nostrils.

"Jumping crickets!" cried O'Madden. "What in tarnation is this…?"

Stretched full-length on the floor in the electric light, with pale bloodless face and inert, apparently unbreathing form, was a disheveled young woman, her unbared left arm displaying a long bloody streak.

IN THE first amazed instant of the discovery, Officer Frye almost lost his grip on Dunbar.

"The saints preserve us! Is she dead?" he gasped.

"Looks like it," concluded O'Madden. "First let's attend to this devil, then we'll investigate."

Out rattled a pair of handcuffs; which clapped themselves about Dunbar's wrists.

Bending down to the girl, Frye felt her forehead. "Why, she's still warm," he discovered. "Couldn't be dead very long."

"You blinking idiots!" raged the captive, struggling in O'Madden's bear-like grip. "What makes you think she's dead? Why, she'll recover soon enough. If you'll give me a chance, I'll bring her back right now. We were just performing a little experiment—"

"Experiment? Like hell!"

It was only then that Frye observed the hypodermic needle on the floor a few feet from the unconscious girl.

"Guess you can tell them all about that down at the station house," he observed, caustically. "Meanwhile we'd better bring the lady down to the doc's office on the first floor. You just keep your grip on that thug, O'Madden…"

Six-foot giant that he was, Frye had gathered the girl into his arms as easily as if she had been a sofa pillow.

"By heavens, if you don't let me go," threatened Dunbar, his black eyes glittering like a crowd of devils dancing, "I swear you'll rue the day…"

Frye's answer was a hoarse burst of laughter.

But cutting through his laughter with the sharpness of an earthquake there came a sudden rattling and banging at the laboratory window. And while the two officers and Knapp stood as if transfixed, the window shade flew up and the window burst open, though there was nothing visible to account for the commotion. O'Madden afterwards asserted that a cold breeze blew by him, though the thermometer stood around 100; and Frye, whose courage no one had ever doubted, did not deny that the hair on his head prickled and a chill swept down his spine...

"IF ONLY it had been something I could have actually seen, no matter what, I would have stood up against it," Frye recited as he told of the event between gulps of a drink made of whisky and soda. "What the devil! A man can only die once! But this thing that you couldn't see or put hands on—Christ, I'd rather fight a herd of stampeding elephants!"

The fact was, as both officers testified, that the very walls of the room shook dramatically, as if rocked to and fro by some mighty unseen force. Dunbar's handcuffs, though O'Madden swore that he had clasped them on firmly, fell to the floor as though they had been mere bands of paper. A decidedly eerie whirring voice, proceeding as if from nowhere, gave warning, "Harm him not, Earthlings, or beware of dire consequences..." And, at the same time, Dunbar was jerked out of the astonished officer's grip!

Yes, jerked away completely, like a toy torn from a child's hands! From the expression on his face, it was evident that Dunbar was as bewildered as anyone as he went gliding toward the window and out—out into the open air, where he disappeared in the fog! While even as he vanished the window shade snapped down and the window slammed shut.

"By glory, the place has got to be haunted," O'Madden had mumbled, crossing himself more than once. And as the three men, with the unconscious girl, had emerged from the outer door of 4E, their faces streamed with a trickling sweat that did not come from the heat alone; and they knew that there was no force on earth powerful enough to induce them to set foot across that threshold again.

CHAPTER TEN
A Plunge in the Dark

BENEATH the great translucent milky-white envelope of the Planetoid, Gates stood in an egg-shaped jelly-like car about thirty feet tall. He was still invisible, even to himself; and could not see the gigantic companion who shared with him his curious vehicle. But through the gelatinous walls he could view the vast cloud-covered expanse of the Earth as it rolled by far beneath.

"Now we must wait, negneg," his unseen companion was saying, "until we whirl around on our orbit to your own part of the globe. Fortunately, it is but a minute planet, and the journey will take scarcely another hour. The instruments will tell us when we arrive. But by my tail! May my brothers not revive before then!"

"What will we do, when we get to Earth?" inquired Gates.

"Do?" hissed Misthrumb. "What do you expect? Why, seek vengeance, as I have told you, Earthling."

"But how will you get this vengeance?"

"You shall see. May the blue lightnings blast me if you do not see. I shall discredit the leadership of the Peerless Red One! I shall frustrate his schemes! I shall invalidate him, as we say on Saturn! Then he will go back home in disgrace, like the scum of the abyss that he is... He will commit Guhl-Guhli—which is to say, he will sting himself to death, and I will come into my own! Then, negneg, I will return and conquer this world as it should be conquered…"

Gates groaned. He began to see that at heart Yellow-Claws was no better than Red-Hood; all he could give the Earth would be a momentary reprieve.

Yet was not even a momentary reprieve better than nothing? This Gates asked himself a little later in a spasm of alarm. Not quite an hour had gone by; and Misthrumb was just preparing to cut the egg-shaped car adrift. But suddenly, through the jelly-like shell of the Planetoid, huge spidery shapes were seen in shadowy movement. And Yellow-Claws whirred with excitement, "Quick, Earthling, quick…or they'll be upon us!"

There came a ripping sound, though no cutting instrument was visible; and the car began to plummet earthward.

But at the same time, through apertures in the walls of the Planetoid, a score of octopus-limbed creatures began to glide, their angry eyes glaring, like triangular rubies, their arms waving fantastically. Around the Planetoid and beneath it they darted, then, gradually becoming dimmer of outline, disappeared from sight.

But Gates was not to be deceived. He knew that they had but garbed themselves in invisibility. He knew that the vibrations given off by Yellow-Claws' body would guide them, although their foe could not be seen. And he was appallingly aware that the whole pack of them were in pursuit of his protector.

"By our planet's ten moons! They must not catch us! If we are captured, we will suffer the penalty of deserters. We will be slain—yes, slain by the method of Multiple Agony, which torments every nerve of the body for many days before death brings relief."

DOWN, down, down they dashed. They rushed through the stratosphere, and the Earth seemed to leap forward to meet them. But reaching the heavier layers of the atmosphere, they were checked by the resistance of the air—and were checked even more by the tangle of invisible Saturnian webs.

Almost at the same time, they were lost in a fog. Whether the Earth was near or far they could not say; they bobbed around like a ship on a stormy sea. "Cursed be all the demons of outer space! Something's wrong with the direction gauge," muttered Yellow-Claws.

Even as he spoke, there came a roar from somewhere near at hand. And a dull-red smoke-puff burst through the fog overhead.

"Fiery imps of Jupiter!" growled Yellow-Claws. "They've got the range!"

It was an extraordinary battle that followed. Both sides were invisible; both aimed frightening flashes in the other's direction. Grimly Gates reflected that Earth-folk, watching the demonstration from below, would think an unusually severe thunderstorm in progress. For in truth there were all the symptoms of a thunderstorm. The sky rumbled with detonations as of gigantic artillery; red, blue and purple lightnings shot through the hazes in zigzag streaks; rain began to fall in howling torrents. How it was that they escaped destruction in that first moment of the encounter was more than Gates could explain; for he saw crimson bars and blue balls of fire playing along the outer surface of the jelly-like envelope.

Manifestly, the car was made of a strongly non-conducting substance; but, even so, he expected the whole fragile affair to collapse instantly.

But the speed of their descent, it soon appeared, was greater than they had imagined; in less than five minutes, they grew conscious of vague outlines just beneath. At almost the same moment, there came a violent threshing and bumping, and Gates, stunned and bruised, was aware of vague projections, which he recognized as the limbs of trees.

At the same time, he was startled by a loud popping, as of a suddenly deflated balloon.

"By the Eleventh Asteroid!" rasped Misthrumb. "We're being torn to shreds!"

Surely enough, the branches of the tree had slashed through the gelatinous envelope, which was hanging from the foliage in wispy, thinly palpitating bands and tatters. Their car—or, rather, all that was left of it—had lodged in the upper limbs of a huge oak, forty feet above ground!

Not that this distance meant anything, so far as Yellow-Claws was concerned. But his protective envelope had been destroyed; and though a red spout of smoke vomited from between his gray-green lips and lunged toward his foe in forked lightnings, he knew that the battle was lost.

"Stay where you are, Earthling," he muttered. "They must not find you. By my fifth arm! They will pay dearly for my life!"

BEFORE these words had died in his ears, Gates knew that Yellow-Claws had sprung down from the tree. The lightnings had become a little more remote, though hardly less terrible. Then a scream shrilled from the distance, and Gates rejoiced to know that one of the enemy had been struck. But almost immediately, closer at hand, there rose an unearthly shriek, followed by a groan as of some being in utmost anguish.

"Thur-glut-nu! Thur-glut-nu!" was shrieked terribly in the Saturnian tongue. And then less fiercely, to Gates.

"May all the devils of the space-ways curse them! They've hit me! Hit me, Earthling, in the middle nerve center!" He referred to a spot beneath the left shoulder, which Gates had learned, was a Saturnian's one really vulnerable point.

Yellow-Claws' next words were rasping and horrible beyond description.

"Flee, negneg, flee! I invoke on them the curses of a thousand dead generations! The venom of all black planets! I—I—by my father's claws, I shall never see Saturn again!"

The cry trailed off into a confusion of words in the sufferer's native tongue. There came another moan; then a series of terrifying snorts, snarls and bellowings, as of a wolfpack closing in on its prey. And red and green lightnings flashed, and blue fireballs played among the treetops...while a pandemonium of thunder drowned out that fiendish chorus.*

Quivering, Gates clung to his perch high in the oak-tree. At any moment, he expected to be snatched up by an invisible arm. Yet time went by, the lightnings and thunders faded out, and at last he began to breathe more easily. He heard the threshing as of mighty forms moving past him. They brushed by the tree; they whisked through

----

* On Earth, fireballs can travel along a wire fence, but are grounded instantly they come to a wooden post, provided they are in direct contact. However, these unearthly fireballs seem to have a negative quality. —Ed.

the woods to right and to left. But thanks to his invisibility, thanks also to the fact that, unlike Misthrumb, he set up no etheric vibration that his enemies could detect, he remained unmolested.

It seemed a long while before at last all became quiet. Then, as the immediate danger passed, the rescued man began to take stock of his position.

"By heavens," he reflected, with a wry grimace, "I'd better not start crowing just yet!" For had he escaped only in order to face a lingering, more cruel doom? Lost in some unknown corner of the woods, perhaps many miles from home; invisible, and without food, money, or other means of making his way, he was, to say the least, in a desperate state. Would he be able, despite all handicaps, to make his way to civilization before Dunbar could carry out his Mephistophelean plots?

His teeth bit into his lower lip with a grimness of determination as, in the misty twilight, he felt his way down from the tree and began searching for an outlet from the wilderness.

CHAPTER ELEVEN
The Electronic Space Ray

THE story of Officers Frye and O'Madden was greeted at the station with incredulous smiles. Evidently these two doughty old members of the force had been drinking too heavily; or else, like so many thousands, had gone crazy with the heat. Nevertheless, thanks to their allegations, two of their brother officers were dispatched to investigate Philip Dunbar's apartment.

An hour later, they returned. Their uniforms were rumpled; their hair lay loose and disheveled across their sweaty red brows; their eyes practically popped from their heads, and their hands shook and twitched with nervous palpitations. Their experience was thus reported to Captain Donnelley by Officer Halloran:

"We went up to that hell's nest, and worse luck to us! Got in without any trouble, didn't we, Jensen? Somebody pulled the door open, and said in the doggonest funniest voice you ever heard, 'Come in, Earthlings, we want some sport!' We knew then there was bats in somebody's belfry, but went in anyway, and would you b'lieve it, there wasn't nobody near the door. We walked further inside, and saw a guy working over a lot of tubes and bottles; he said his name was Dunbar all right, and yelled at us, 'I warn you, get out, before it's too late!'

" 'We've got a warrant for your arrest,' says I, 'so you'd better come nice and quiet.' At that he just laughed, didn't he, Jensen?"

"You'd of thought it was something funny, being arrested, by jiminy!" affirmed Officer Jensen.

"Well, nobody wouldn't ever believe it, but before I could get to the guy, the handcuffs was knocked right outa my hands," went on Halloran. "Not by that fellow Dunbar, neither. He was over on the other side of the room. Somebody hit me right through the air, with something I couldn't see. May I be boiled in tar if I lie!"

"You sure oughter be boiled in tar, if you expect me to believe that tommyrot," growled the Captain.

"Well, b'lieve it or not, that ain't nothing to what happened to me," Jensen took up the story. "I felt something grabbing me by the hair. Yes, so help me God! I reached up my hand, and felt something cold and hard, like a lobster's claw. But you still couldn't see a damned thing!"

"Shoulda' heard what a yell Jensen let out," Halloran continued. "Sure was fit to wake the dead!"

"Oh, gwan!" countered Jensen. "'Twasn't nothing to the way you hollered when you was pitched plumb across the room!"

"Well, who wouldn't holler if they was batted hard against the wall by some invisible devil? I ain't boasting when I say I'm a tough nut to crack, but when that thing, whatever it was, began tweaking my ears and nose and saying, 'This is the way we'll twist your necks, Earthlings, if the likes of you ever come back here'—well then, what in thunder do you think I'd do? Stay to get my neck twisted?"

The Captain meanwhile was smiling cynically.

"You boys sure must think I like fish stories," he remarked.

It may not be that anyone took Jensen and Halloran quite seriously. Yet was it not hard to believe that four trusty old members of the force had all gone crazy? The fact is, in any case, that when the Captain considered sending two more men to the mysterious apartment, he could find no one who did not threaten to resign from the force sooner than accept the assignment.

ELEANOR meanwhile, as Dunbar had predicted, had regained consciousness. Yet she could give only a confused account of what had happened. "When the bell began ringing so furiously," she testified, "I thought I heard someone sneaking up behind me, but as I turned I suddenly felt a sharp jab in one arm. By then it was too late even to cry out. Everything went black around me before I'd even had time to realize Dunbar had stabbed me with a hypodermic."

Thanks to her entreaties and the testimony of the officers, she was granted a bodyguard of two detectives; for, as she asserted, "The minute I walk out by myself, that fiend will recapture me. And I have work to do—very important work, if the world is to be saved..."

Everyone smiled in half-veiled amusement. Yet no one could deny the deadly seriousness of the girl's manner.

No one could deny, either, that she was in danger from some mysterious source. On the day after her release, two men in a taxicab swerved suddenly around a street corner, and came within an inch of snatching her from under the noses of the detectives. The would-be abductors, though unsuccessful, made good their escape; and later that same day a still more ominous event occurred.

Eleanor was walking in a fog not far from one of the city's main intersections, when suddenly she felt something clutching her. She cried out in terror; and the detectives, though seeing nothing, fired into the mist. Evidently it was a mere lucky shot that struck the unseen aggressor under the left shoulder, at his "middle nerve center," his most vulnerable spot. At any rate, an unearthly howl came from the invisible—and, more significant yet, a spout of something thick, sticky, and golden-orange jutted to the pavement as if from nowhere. And the girl felt the claws of the invisible beast relaxing.

"Another damned attack of nerves," Police Captain Donnelley called it when the incident was reported. Yet, being unable to account for the golden-yellow liquid, he consented to double the girl's bodyguard.

Knowing that the time was exceedingly short—in fact, to take Dunbar's word for it, only four days of grace remained—she worked with desperation. Her first idea was to obtain possession of Gates' infra-red eye, which might show the authorities the cobweb meshes that entangled the planet, and so perhaps rouse them to eleventh hour action. But obtaining this invaluable device was a mystery. Neither a search of the laboratory, nor a ransacking of Gates' home revealed any trace of the instrument. Eleanor remembered in despair how, on that memorable evening on the roof, the inventor dropped the device just as the Saturnians swooped down; and she concluded that it had either been broken, lost, or snatched up by the invaders.

THEREFORE she turned to her one other hope. For almost a year during her spare hours in the laboratory, she had been working on what she called the Electronic Space Ray—a beam designed to pierce and dissolve the upper cloud formations. This ray, which was a modification of the X-ray, engendered by an application of several hundred thousand volts of electricity, had the power of cutting like a knife through any mist, causing the vapors to disperse as though blown aside by a gale. Its range, apparently, was enormous; Eleanor believed it capable of bridging the gulf from the Earth to the moon, and held that it would be highly effective at several hundred miles.

Therefore the question arose: if the rays could dissipate a cloud, could they not penetrate the gelatinous envelopes of the Crystal Planetoids? Was it not conceivable that they could rip the Planetoids apart, as a balloon may be ripped by a bullet? She did not know, but the chance, however fantastic it seemed, was not to be ignored.

Surrounded by her four guards, she hastened to the laboratory of the Merlin Research Institute; and, requiring solitude for efficient work, busied herself from dawn to dusk and even through the early hours of daylight to perfect her invention. Formerly she had expected to be able to finish the contrivance at her leisure. But now with what feverish haste she labored, scarcely taking time to eat, to sleep, to think except of one thing only.

At first the fear haunted her that the Saturnians would break in and steal her away despite her bodyguard. But was it that the one lucky shot, which had spilled the golden-orange blood of her attacker, had deterred the invaders? More probably, they did not think her worth bothering about—what could she, one poor feeble woman, do to avert the doom that had been so well-plotted, and that was so soon to descend?

The heat, as she worked, had risen to furnace intensity. Temperatures below a hundred were now rarely found near sea level in the so-called temperate regions; all breezes, except those engendered by electric fans, were memories of the dear departed days; while so many areas were parched and browned, so many people were perishing on all sides, that bureau of statistics no longer kept records. That the long awaited Day of Judgment was at hand; that the destruction of the Earth and all its inhabitants was a matter but of weeks or at most of months, was now the theme of preachers and laymen alike; millions, ceasing to hope, passed their days amid a long mumbling of lamentations and prayers.

MEANWHILE few knew or cared about the young woman who, with eyes red and strained, with fingers deft yet nervously hurried, with skin and lab apron mottled with chemicals, yet with a spirit that refused to give up, labored amid the motors and ray-spouting tubes, the flasks and crucibles of the steamy hot laboratory. Nearly five days had gone by before she had put her machine into working order—five days that, in view of the time lost under the spell of the hypodermic drug, should bring her beyond the deadline set by Dunbar. Already, perhaps, he had turned over the containers of compressed air to the Saturnians! Already they were making their last deadly assault. Already it was too late—too late to save the Earth!

Nevertheless, if but one chance in ten thousand remained, that chance must not be cast aside.

Her machine, when ready, was a monstrous-looking affair, somewhat resembling a siege-gun in appearance. The fifteen-foot steel snout, shooting upward like a spire from the central mass of lenses, prisms and radio-like tubes, was attached by wires to several huge dynamos. A telescope, fastened to the side of the main tube, connected with the range-finder; while the whole could be moved hither and thither on wheels, a little like a great gun on its carriage.

Three skilled mechanics, who had helped to construct the apparatus on Eleanor's instructions, shook their heads doubtfully over the completed instrument. "The lady must be crazy," they muttered in private, "if she thinks such a rigamagig can save the world."

The skeptics were, it is true, somewhat impressed by the first demonstration. The machine was wheeled into a courtyard adjoining the Research Institute; and its mouth was pointed upward into the mists that precluded visibility above a hundred feet. At a signal, the power was turned on; there came a low whirring, accompanied by blue flashes; and almost instantly, as if some unseen fist had thrust its way through them, the vapors disappeared from a circle of sky about ten degrees across, and the azure of heaven appeared for the first time in many days.

Equally impressive was the next experiment. A number of open jars of gelatin were placed against the walls of the building, and the machine was pointed toward them. For half a dozen seconds they were bombarded by the rays; then, upon examination, the gelatin was found to have vanished—to have dissolved despite the intervening glass of the jars, which themselves had seemingly been unaffected!

A faint glow of hope came to the girl's mind as she witnessed these results. Could it be, after all, that not everything was as hopeless as it seemed? A machine that could work such miracles might also perform wonders against the Planetoids!

But even as this thought flashed over her, there came another realization—a numb, dull realization that struck her like a hand of lead. On one of the Planetoids, hundreds if not thousands of humans were held—at least, so she judged from the reports of the many that disappeared mysteriously after setting out to see Gates dangled from the web of the invaders. Worst of all! The man she loved was a prisoner! If she destroyed the Planetoids, she would destroy Ronald! And after that, though, the world lived on, what meaning would life have for her?

But only for the barest of moments did she hesitate. They had reached a point where the fate of individuals did not matter. The sacrifice of all the captives, lamentable as it would be—the sacrifice of her lover—the sacrifice of herself—what did all this count beside the future of the human race?

Gritting her teeth and clenching her fists, she turned back to the Electronic Space Ray. Her eyes were desolate but her manner was determined as she picked up the range finder and revolved the telescope through a newly cleared circle of blue sky.

CHAPTER TWELVE
Prelude to Battle

THERE are some grave disadvantages in being invisible. So, at least, Gates concluded as he went groping through the woods in the effort to find his bearings. It is disconcerting, to say the least, to ask a passer-by the way, and to be greeted with a shriek, and watch the man turn and dash away frantically, as from a ghost. It is aggravating to reach an automobile road and find every car trying to drive full-tilt through you. Gates felt like a man returning from the dead as he picked his way out of the woods, and reaching a village, began to make a few civil inquiries... Inevitably, he found, his hearers would flee the vicinity of his voice; and the harder he tried to call them back the faster they would run.

He passed the night in an open field under a haystack—which, considering the heat, was not at all a hardship. In the morning, driven by hunger, he strolled into a farmhouse; and while the family stampeded like sheep from the sound of his footsteps, he calmly helped himself to some ham and biscuits from the kitchen table. Having thus satisfied his needs, he wandered away along a railroad track, and after about an hour's walk reached a junction, where a sign on the station showed him that he was two hundred miles from home. "How am I ever going to make the distance?" he wondered, reflecting that he had not a penny in his pockets.

Twenty minutes later, while he still stood there baffled, a train puffed into the station—one of the few still running in those disorganized days. Several people stepped aboard; and, without hesitation, he joined them, trusting to his invisibility to save him from the demands of the ticket-taker.

As there was no unoccupied seat, he stood in the vestibule, which caused not a little confusion, as people kept brushing against him as they went by, greatly to their consternation. Long before they had reached their destination, in fact, half the passengers were ready to swear that the train was haunted. This view was furthered by Buck Johnson, one of the colored waiters in the dining car, who testified that while his back was turned the better part of the contents of a tray disappeared—and that he turned about just in time to see a sausage go floating down the passageway, although nobody was in sight!

It was fortunate, Gates thought, that the train was air-conditioned; the cool, fresh atmosphere made it easier for him to think. And, certainly, he needed to think as never before. What would he do upon getting back home? Obviously, go as soon as possible to Dunbar's apartment, to check that traitor's vile designs, if there were still time! And to rescue Eleanor from his clutches. But was it not already too late? Gates gravely feared so. Besides, how could he prevail against Dunbar, protected as he was by the overweening power of the Saturnians?

"Well, at least," Gates reflected, "I can't be seen—that's one strategic advantage." But it would take more than his invisibility to win the battle. He must have weapons—weapons of unrivalled power. And where could such be found?

AT this thought he remembered a certain invention he had toyed with months before. It was a knife that he called the Electric Blade: a folding strip of metal, small and compact, and short enough to be carried in a man's hip pocket, yet capable of being extended to the length of one's forearm, where it would cut with the sharpness of a sword. To it was attached a minute but powerful storage battery that Gates had perfected, a battery that made it possible for the blade to slash back and forth with such swiftness that the naked eye could hardly follow its motions. The inventor had believed that the weapon might prove valuable for close combat work in warfare; but had lost interest in it temporarily while working on that still more important device, the Infra-Red Eye.

It was, however, with the greatest of enthusiasm that he thought now of the Electric Blade. Might this not be just what he needed in the conflict with Dunbar? Knowing something of the prowess of the Saturnians, he was far from sure; nevertheless, he swore a bitter oath, "I'll have a try at it, even if they hack me to mincemeat!"—which, he realized, they were only too likely to do.

The Electric Blade, he recalled, had been left in his locker at the Merlin Research Institute. Accordingly, it was to this spot that he must hasten immediately upon returning to the city.

It was night by the time he had reached the building; and the front door was locked. But seeing a light inside, he rapped. As no answer came, he rapped again, this time more loudly; and then rapped once more, still more loudly. It was only after the fourth or fifth summons that he heard shuffling footsteps warily approaching. "What the devil!" he muttered to himself. "Do they think I want to steal the building?"

"Who's there?" a voice from within demanded, huskily.

"It's Ronald Gates, an employee of the Institute…"

There was a momentary hesitation. He heard two men conferring in whispers; then the door opened a few inches, and he stared into the muzzle of a revolver, behind which glowered the grim, determined face of a uniformed man.

"Don't be scared, Officer," he began, slightly amused. "I can establish my identity—"

Instantly there rang out a yell from the uniformed man. Savagely the door banged to a close. "By God! It's one of them devils from Saturn!"

Almost simultaneously, he heard another voice taking up the cry. "Run, Miss, run! Quick! Ain't no time to waste! One of them fiends is after you again!"

From within, he heard a woman's scream. "Out this way! This way!" And all other sounds were lost amid the scurrying of feet.

But had those tones not had a familiar ring? Could it be—or was his heated imagination only playing tricks?

HE lost no time, however, in useless questionings. Realizing that the fugitives must leave by the rear exit, on another street, he raced around the block in such haste that he bowled over two pedestrians who were never to know what had hit them. As he approached the rear door, he saw five figures hurriedly emerge, among them a young woman, the sight of whom caused his heart to pound furiously.

"Eleanor!" he shouted. "Eleanor!"

The girl glanced toward him, and shrieked. Even if she recognized his voice, she undoubtedly thought that it was merely one of the Saturnians imitating him.

"Eleanor! Eleanor!" he repeated. "It's Ronald! It's me!"

But it was doubtful if she even heard. Preceding the four policemen—pushed and shoved by them, for he had never seen men in more frantic haste—she was lost to view inside a black sedan. A moment later, the car had spurted from sight around the corner.

Greatly shaken, Gates returned to the Institute. It was much—very much—to know that Eleanor was alive, and apparently not in Dunbar's hands. But to have her flee him as though he was a plague-bearer; to be mistaken by her for one of the Saturnians—that was a new and totally unexpected experience. Now, as never before, he began to curse his invisibility.

But there was work to be done—work from which he must not be deterred even by the thought of Eleanor. And at this point, as if by way of compensation, his invisibility served him to excellent purpose. How, considering that the doors were all locked, could he get into the institute? Contemplatively he strolled around the building and saw that the one possible entry was by means of an open window facing the fire escape on the third floor. To hoist himself up to the fire escape was, to be sure, no great task for one of his agility; but as it gave upon a main street, where many people were passing, it would have been impossible for any ordinary man to accomplish the feat without detection. As it was, however, he managed the entry with ease.

Once within, he made his way down to the locker room, where he switched on the lights, and turned to his own locker—the combination of which, fortunately, had not been altered. A moment later, the door rattled open. He saw that the interior had been disturbed, as though somebody had entered during his absence and fumbled among the contents; but his pulse pounded with excitement when, safely hidden in a corner, he located a steel-sheathed apparatus of about the size of a large pistol.

"Thank heaven," he muttered. "This little blade may hold the world's destiny…"

He placed the instrument carefully beneath his garments, so that it too became invisible. He then closed the locker and started away with the knowledge that he hastened to a battle that could end only in victory or death.

CHAPTER THIRTEEN
The Electric Blade Swings

STRIPPED to the waist, Philip Dunbar worked in the electric glare of the oven-hot laboratory. The throbbing of motors made a dull undertone in his ears as he examined the register connecting with the steel cylinders of compressed air. His dark face had become long and haggard; his eyes glittered with a wild, almost demoniacal light. But a grunt of satisfaction came from between those two thin cynic lips of his as he muttered,

"Thank the Lord. At last it's done..."

"Thank not the Lord, Earthling. Thank us!" a whirring voice sounded from just outside the window. "For many days we have followed your labors. For many days we have assisted. Nevertheless, you are a day behind schedule. A whole day, Earthling..."

"I have done my best!" sighed Dunbar. "Could I help it if I was sick with the heat for two days and could hardly work?"

"We will forgive you this once, negneg, although on our planet we are not such weaklings as to get...sick. After all, you have served us not badly. Tomorrow, with the compressed air to improve our efficiency, we will be lords of this world."

"Tomorrow we will be lords of this world!" another voice, from an all invisible source, weirdly repeated.

"Earthling, we have one more command," buzzed the first voice. "These casks of compressed air are hard for us to reach through your narrow window. See that they are placed outside on the ground. Have them put there early tomorrow, that we may gather them up with ease."

"I shall do so," acceded Dunbar, and hastily he added, "Then you will not—will not forget your promise?"

"Never fear..." a voice of reassurance droned. "When all the rest of your race sleeps in the long Forever, you will be glad to be alive—you, the last man."

"I will be glad to be alive," acknowledged Dunbar. But his voice had a tone of sadness; his long, lean, dark countenance drooped.

"One thing more...the female of my race...the girl I call Eleanor—have you not saved her as a reward for my services? Through the wiles of wicked connivers she has escaped. Once more I ask you, can you not seize her and bring her back?"

"Once more I tell you, Earthling, the Peerless Red One has changed his mind about the female of your species. In truth, we were not sorry when she got away; and made but little effort to recapture her, for she drew your mind from your work. The Peerless Red One has decided if the female of the species is crafty enough to get away, might she not be crafty enough to cause us much trouble? No, Earthling. Let her perish with the rest of her crawling species!"

Dunbar groaned; and sank disconsolately to the laboratory floor. Had he not learned that nothing was more futile than to argue with a Saturnian?

THE dreary gray of dawn was visible through the stagnant cloud-banks by the time Gates had started toward Dunbar's apartment.

One thing in particular had delayed him. Having secured the Electric Blade, he decided that he must also obtain the Infra-Red Eye as a precaution in case of conflict with the Saturnians. One of the instruments, he recalled to his regret, had been lost during that first encounter with the invaders from space. But there was another, which he had left for safekeeping in the home of his old friend, a man named Bill Denny. Here, however, was indeed a predicament—how could he get to Denny and ask for his property, now that he was invisible? After much thought, he concluded that only one course was open to him; hence, taking a flashlight from his locker at the Institute, he hurried to Bill Denny's home, climbed in through a window, and began to ransack his friend's spare room, where he knew the Infra-Red Eye was kept.

It was this that gave rise to panic in the Denny household, bringing forth Martha Denny's screams when she awakened long after midnight to discover a light proceeding as if on its own volition down an empty hallway. Bill Denny, who went to investigate, said that he heard the sound of racing footsteps and saw a gleam, which he attributed to a burglar's flashlight. This theory was borne out the following morning by the disordered state of the spare room. But what nobody could understand was that a bill-packed wallet, which stood in plain sight, had been untouched; while the only thing taken was the peculiar-looking contraption entrusted to Denny weeks before by his missing friend, poor old Ronny Gates.

Meantime, with the Infra-Red Eye shielded from sight beneath his garments, Gates was approaching Dunbar's apartment house. As he drew near in the early dawn, he paused in an adjoining court; and a thrill of satisfaction shot through him to know that, after all, he was not too late. No! But he was barely in time, for two workmen, heaving and panting, were throwing a thick steel cylinder on top of a great heap.

Beside them stood Dunbar, looking hot and unhappy as he directed their movements with nervous haste. "Now you fellows, just one more," he was ordering with a slight growl. "Go up and get it, and I'll pay you off. Go on, quick—what are you such snails about?"

As the men slouched away, Gates let out an unconscious grunt; at which Dunbar turned sharply toward, terror in his piercing black little eyes. "Good heavens…" he muttered to himself as he hastily lit a cigarette. "I'm getting so I see things everywhere…"

A FEW minutes later, the last of the cylinders had been deposited on the heap; the workmen had been paid, and had gone shuffling off. Dunbar, leaning against the pile, was awaiting the arrival of the Saturnians. Nor had he long to wait. The laborers had hardly passed out of sight around the corner when one of the cylinders began to move as of its own will, and with gradually accelerating velocity, shot into the air and out of sight.

Now if ever, Gates realized, was the time to act! With trembling speed, he drew the Infra-Red Eye from under his coat, so as to reveal the Saturnians who, he felt sure, were all about him. For a moment alarm possessed him; for the Eye, being visible, would betray him to the foe! But no…evidently some of the residue Amvol-Amvol had been rubbed upon it in its contact with his clothes; it too seemed to be invisible.

Hastily he adjusted it, by means of tight bands running around his head; yet not so hastily as to make unnecessary noise. How fortunate, he thought, that the Saturnians' ears were less acute than some of their other senses! Yet what he saw, after he had turned the proper screws and levers, was nothing to reassure him. Not one Saturnian, nor even two, as he had expected! Nor even five or six! At least twelve of the great creatures, with their dangling octopus limbs, their long stinging tails, their red triangular eyes—at least twelve of them, all seeming of a watery pallor through the Infra-Red Eye! And among them, leading them as he strutted savagely back and forth among the compressed air containers, was the over-towering form of the Peerless Red One!

Pressed into a basement doorway for protection, Gates planned his action. His mind worked with spring-like rapidity; he knew that he had not a second to waste. Two advantages were his: the Electric Blade, and his ability to take his adversaries by surprise. But how slight these assets seemed by comparison with the number and prowess of his foes!

Yet not for an instant did he flinch. If he must die, then he must die... Out from beneath his coat came the Electric Blade, its sheath fortunately invisible: but after he had set the motors into operation, the whirring sound betrayed him.

"What's that?" came suspiciously from one of the Saturnians, in his native tongues, as the monster started toward the source of the sound.

Instantly Gates released the blade to its full length. But, as he did so, he received another shock. The metal, in its folded position, had evidently missed contact with the Amvol-Amvol! It could be seen just like any ordinary steel!

"Ah! What devil have we here?" dinned from the Saturnian, in a mighty roar. And he lunged in Gates' direction.

AS he did so, the blade began to swing with such speed that it made but a gray blur. Too swift for the Saturnians to follow its movements, the steel slashed at the assailant, whom Gates could clearly see through the Infra-Red Eye. The first blows made but minor dents in the creature's tough armor; but after a second or two Gates swung the weapon upward toward the enemy's left shoulder.

Horrible to hear was the monster's howl as the Middle Nerve Center was penetrated and fountains of golden-orange overflowed the pavement. Terrible beyond words was his death-yell as he sagged and sank, and, with all his limbs threshing violently, clutched blindly for his foe.

But Gates had leapt out of range. Vehemently he was darting hither and thither among the Saturnians, slashing in all directions with the furiously swinging blade. He could see the octopus limbs of half a score of the creatures writhing simultaneously toward him, interfering with one another in their conclusive movements. However, they aimed not at him but at the blade, and always they struck at the point where it had been just a fraction of a second before their blows descended. Thus, by a hair's breadth, Gates was able to elude them.

How long would he be able to keep up the unequal struggle? His strength was waning; his breath was coming hard and fast; its very sound would have betrayed him had it not been for the other noises of battle. Already he had wounded several adversaries, though not mortally; their golden-yellow blood flowed, but they still fought on. Time after time he felt himself brushed by their sweeping arms; felt their deathly cold claws against his skin. Once, by less than a finger's breadth, he escaped a lashing envenomed tail.

Even as he lodged this peril, Gates recognized the huge gray-green lips of Red-Hood. He saw the malevolent red light in the eyes of his chief antagonist; and, like a matador fleeing a bull, he ducked and ran sideways. Then, with ferocious suddenness, he turned and swung the flashing blade upward.

A fraction of a second too soon or too late, and he would have been lost. A few inches too high, or a few inches too low, and he might as well not have fought at all. But Red-Hood, stooping low as he charged head forward, had exposed the vulnerable left shoulder. And straight through the susceptible spot burst the cleaving, electrically driven blade.

RED-HOOD'S roar of rage and agony, as he sank amid hideous convulsions, was all but drowned by the dismayed bellowings of his companions. One and all, as though they had hit a blank wall, halted in shrieking consternation at the awareness of their smitten leader. And Gates, springing forward, profited from that instant of demoralization, to strike another of the creatures through the Middle Nerve Center.

As he leapt back, barely in time to avert the drive of the swinging tail, he made an amazing observation. The creatures were all in flight! From their terrorized cries, he surmised that they thought they were fighting not one man, but an invisible army!

But the last of the monsters, as he turned to flee, swung back briefly. Crouched in a cranny against a coal-bin, was a cowering form, its eyes wide with terror. "You, negneg— you, you are the root of all our trouble!" rasped the Saturnian. "You have betrayed us! You shall be punished!"

Out swung the terrible tail; its barbed point, with the speed of an arrow, plunged into Dunbar's heart. And as the victim, gasping, collapsed in his own blood, his assailant went swinging away up a great cobweb.

Meanwhile Gates, sinking in exhaustion to the pavement, stared at the stones smeared with great streaks of golden-yellow; stared at the still untouched containers of compressed air, and solemnly mumbled a prayer of thanksgiving.

CHAPTER FOURTEEN
Deliverance

GATES' first thought, after recovering his breath, was to finish his half-completed task. What if the Saturnian retreat was but temporary? What if the foe should rally, and return with redoubled fury? What if, after all, they should seize the containers of compressed air, and so accomplish their original purpose and conquer the planet?

"By glory...not if I can prevent it," Gates swore a secret oath, as he staggered toward the great steel cylinders. To carry off even one of the heavy affairs would, obviously, be impossible—but was there no other way? After a swift examination, he noticed a little faucet-like spout at the end of one of the vessels, and took it to be a valve to relieve excessive pressure.

"Just five minutes leeway," he thought, "and there won't be a whiff of compressed air left..."

At the same time, he gave the spigot a swift turn in his fingers.

Instantly there came such a blast that he was stunned. A loud popping, as of an explosion, dinned in his ears. He reeled backward, knocked over as if by a hurricane. For a second or two a great fury of escaping air blew by him.

Still a little dazed, he picked himself up moments later, cursing his own stupidity. In his haste he had turned the vent on full force, so relieving far too much pressure—with results that might have been disastrous.

Worst of all, what if the commotion should summon the Saturnians back?

Even as this fear swept across him, he made a discovery, which for the moment alarmed him even more. He could see himself again! His arms, his legs, and all of his body, were perfectly visible! The blast of air had been powerful enough to blow away most of the Amvol-Amvol, the powder of invisibility!

Aware that he would be utterly at the Saturnians' mercy should they return, he worked as quickly as humanly possible to release the compressed air from the other containers. At any moment he expected to be snatched up by a swooping giant claw and borne away to his doom. But time went by and the monsters did not re-appear. At length the last of the compressed air cylinders was empty...

Then for the first time, as he started hastily away, a flash of joyous realization swept over him. What a relief to be visible again! Once more he could be received as a man.

EARLY IN THE morning hours not long after the alarm from the supposed Saturnians—actually Gates—Eleanor insisted on returning to her work with the Electronic Space Ray. Surrounded by a whole squad of burly policemen—since her four previous protectors had strenuously insisted that they were too few—she entered the courtyard adjoining the Research Institute where her machine, with its fifteen-foot cannon-like muzzle, was pointed skyward. Now at last she was ready for the crucial work!

Reaching the courtyard, she adjusted the instrument; cleared an open circle of blue sky; and in so doing completely destroyed, she knew, an incalculable number of the invisible cobwebs that had been clogging up the atmosphere. But she was out after bigger prey than cobwebs. By means of the telescope she located a tiny shining speck which she recognized as one of the Crystal Planetoids; and, with trembling hands, pointed her machine toward the section of the sky containing the Planetoid.

Then, for the barest fraction of a second, she hesitated. She knew it was but a womanly weakness; she knew it was unworthy of her, inconsistent with her all-important scheme; yet the hot tears trickled quickly down her cheeks, and something clutched at the back of her throat. The next flick of her fingers might be the movement that destroyed scores of human beings, among them Ronny, her lover.

Nevertheless, she held back only for the briefest of instants. Her fingers flashed against a lever; and a faint clicking came to her ears. With eyes glued to the telescope, she watched; and immediately it seemed, she made out a puff of red fire where the Planetoid had been—a puff that swiftly gave way to long ruddy streamers, which almost as swiftly vanished.

Still struggling, she could not hold back her sobs any longer. "I know Ronny would forgive me if somehow he knew," she consoled herself. Nevertheless, several minutes had passed, before, with a great effort of will, she turned to the range finder, and prepared to look for another Planetoid.

Then it was, that all at once there came a sound, which she heard, in mute, incredulous amazement. What was that voice...that familiar, exultant voice arising suddenly behind her? "Eleanor..."

Wheeling about, she faced what she at first mistook for an apparition. Could this be Ronald? This disheveled man with the face ghostly pale, although his eyes were agleam with joy?

But as he strode forward, and flung out his arms, she knew that he was indeed no phantom!

NO LESS surprising than the speed with which the Saturnians had overspread the entire Earth was the rapidity with which the peril now receded. Within a few weeks, while dozens of Electronic Space Rays swept across the heavens to clear away the great alien cobwebs, the temperature of the planet returned to normal ranges; the winds blew and gusted again as usual; the ferocious thunder storms, the floods and the droughts had dwindled to ghastly memories. If any of the monsters still ranged the Earth's surface, they had returned to remote, unpopulated regions; no trace of them was ever seen, except for some mysterious streaks of yellow-orange observed by mariners on an islet not too far from Cape Horn, where the last of the invaders had been dashed to their doom.

As for the Planetoids—so mercilessly were they hunted by the Space Rays that within a matter of days the most careful searching of the heavens failed to reveal even one of the great gelatinous balls. The watchers on Saturn, it was generally agreed, would not be encouraged by the results of their expedition. And if ever they should attempt another invasion, the weapons to repel them would be at hand.

Meantime, while paeans of thanksgiving resounded from all lands, the world's eyes were focused on two individuals. The nuptials of Eleanor Firth and Ronald Gates, which were celebrated a few weeks after the overthrow of the Menace, were the occasion for universal rejoicing, for nothing could have appeared more fitting than the union of these two.

THE END

If you've enjoyed this book, you will not want to miss these terrific titles…

ARMCHAIR SCI-FI & HORROR DOUBLE NOVELS, $12.95 each

D-1   **THE GALAXY RAIDERS** by William P. McGivern
SPACE STATION #1 by Frank Belknap Long

D-2   **THE PROGRAMMED PEOPLE** by Jack Sharkey
SLAVES OF THE CRYSTAL BRAIN by William Carter Sawtelle

D-3   **YOU'RE ALL ALONE** by Fritz Leiber
THE LIQUID MAN by Bernard C. Gilford

D-4   **CITADEL OF THE STAR LORDS** by Edmond Hamilton
VOYAGE TO ETERNITY by Milton Lesser

D-5   **IRON MEN OF VENUS** by Don Wilcox
THE MAN WITH ABSOLUTE MOTION by Noel Loomis

D-6   **WHO SOWS THE WIND…** by Rog Phillips
THE PUZZLE PLANET by Robert A. W. Lowndes

D-7   **PLANET OF DREAD** by Murray Leinster
TWICE UPON A TIME by Charles L. Fontenay

D-8   **THE TERROR OUT OF SPACE** by Dwight V. Swain
QUEST OF THE GOLDEN APE by Ivar Jorgensen and Adam Chase

D-9   **SECRET OF MARRACOTT DEEP** by Henry Slesar
PAWN OF THE BLACK FLEET by Mark Clifton.

D-10   **BEYOND THE RINGS OF SATURN** by Robert Moore Williams
A MAN OBSESSED by Alan E. Nourse

ARMCHAIR SCIENCE FICTION CLASSICS, $12.95 each

C-1   **THE GREEN MAN**
by Harold M. Sherman

C-2   **A TRACE OF MEMORY**
By Keith Laumer

C-3   **INTO PLUTONIAN DEPTHS**
by Stanton A. Coblentz

ARMCHAIR MASTERS OF SCIENCE FICTION SERIES, $16.95 each

M-1   **MASTERS OF SCIENCE FICTION, Vol. One**
Bryce Walton—"Dark of the Moon" and other tales

M-2   **MASTERS OF SCIENCE FICTION, Vol. Two**
Jerome Bixby—"One Way Street" and other tales

If you've enjoyed this book, you will not want to miss these terrific titles…

ARMCHAIR SCI-FI & HORROR DOUBLE NOVELS, $12.95 each

D-11 **PERIL OF THE STARMEN** by Kris Neville
THE STRANGE INVASION by Murray Leinster

D-12 **THE STAR LORD** by Boyd Ellanby
CAPTIVES OF THE FLAME by Samuel R. Delany

D-13 **MEN OF THE MORNING STAR** by Edmond Hamilton
PLANET FOR PLUNDER by Hal Clement and Sam Merwin, Jr.

D-14 **ICE CITY OF THE GORGON** by Chester S. Geier and Richard Shaver
WHEN THE WORLD TOTTERED by Lester del Rey

D-15 **WORLDS WITHOUT END** by Clifford D. Simak
THE LAVENDER VINE OF DEATH by Don Wilcox

D-16 **SHADOW ON THE MOON** by Joe Gibson
ARMAGEDDON EARTH by Geoff St. Reynard

D-17 **THE GIRL WHO LOVED DEATH** by Paul W. Fairman
SLAVE PLANET by Laurence M. Janifer

D-18 **SECOND CHANCE** by J. F. Bone
MISSION TO A DISTANT STAR by Frank Belknap Long

D-19 **THE SYNDIC** by C. M. Kornbluth
FLIGHT TO FOREVER by Poul Anderson

D-20 **SOMEWHERE I'LL FIND YOU** by Milton Lesser
THE TIME ARMADA by Fox B. Holden

ARMCHAIR SCIENCE FICTION CLASSICS, $12.95 each

C-4 **CORPUS EARTHLING**
by Louis Charbonneau

C-5 **THE TIME DISSOLVER**
by Jerry Sohl

C-6 **WEST OF THE SUN**
by Edgar Pangborn

ARMCHAIR SCI-FI & HORROR GEMS SERIES, $12.95 each

G-1 **SCIENCE FICTION GEMS, Vol. One**
Isaac Asimov and others

G-2 **HORROR GEMS, Vol. One**
Carl Jacobi and others

If you've enjoyed this book, you will not want to miss these terrific titles…

ARMCHAIR SCI-FI & HORROR DOUBLE NOVELS, $12.95 each

D-21   **EMPIRE OF EVIL** by Robert Arnette
       THE SIGN OF THE TIGER by Alan E. Nourse & J. A. Meyer

D-22   **OPERATION SQUARE PEG** by Frank Belknap Long
       ENCHANTRESS OF VENUS by Leigh Brackett

D-23   **THE LIFE WATCH** by Lester del Rey
       CREATURES OF THE ABYSS by Murray Leinster

D-24   **LEGION OF LAZARUS** by Edmond Hamilton
       STAR HUNTER by Andre Norton

D-25   **EMPIRE OF WOMEN** by John Fletcher
       ONE OF OUR CITIES IS MISSING by Irving Cox

D-26   **THE WRONG SIDE OF PARADISE** by Raymond F. Jones
       THE INVOLUNTARY IMMORTALS by Rog Phillips

D-27   **EARTH QUARTER** by Damon Knight
       ENVOY TO NEW WORLDS by Keith Laumer

D-28   **SLAVES TO THE METAL HORDE** by Milton Lesser
       HUNTERS OUT OF TIME by Joseph E. Kelleam

D-29   **RX JUPITER SAVE US** by Ward Moore
       BEWARE THE USURPERS by Geoff St. Reynard

D-30   **SECRET OF THE SERPENT** by Don Wilcox
       CRUSADE ACROSS THE VOID by Dwight V. Swain

ARMCHAIR SCIENCE FICTION CLASSICS, $12.95 each

C-7   **THE SHAVER MYSTERY, Book One**
       by Richard S. Shaver

C-8   **THE SHAVER MYSTERY, Book Two**
       by Richard S. Shaver

C-9   **MURDER IN SPACE**
       by David V. Reed

ARMCHAIR MASTERS OF SCIENCE FICTION SERIES, $16.95 each

M-3   **MASTERS OF SCIENCE FICTION, Vol. Three**
       Robert Sheckley, "The Perfect Woman" and other tales

M-4   **MASTERS OF SCIENCE FICTION, Vol. Four**
       Mack Reynolds, Part One, "Stowaway" and other tales

A RENDEZVOUS WITH THE PAST...

Try to imagine what it would be like to suddenly lose control of your body, with your legs and arms no longer at your command. Then try to imagine what it would be like to lose control of your mind, with strange thoughts and words suddenly spewing forth. It sounds a little far-fetched, but this was exactly what was happening to Don King—and it almost drove him mad! Next had come the wanderlust, an uncontrollable urge to visit far-away countries—but why? What was he searching for? He soon turned to a psychiatrist for help. Together they searched for the key that might unlock the bizarre mystery his mind and body were going through. But in truth, Don King was the reincarnation of a man who had lived 11,000 years ago—which wasn't so odd in and of itself, except that the man was still alive and kicking!

CAST OF CHARACTERS

DON KING
He felt a "calling" that led him all over the world, searching for the key that would unlock a strange mystery within himself.

SONTHIA
Probably the best-looking 11,000-year old girl on Earth. Friendly, too—all she wanted to do was overthrow her kingdom's ruler.

DOR DIAVO
He was a merciless tyrant with a lust for blood. He also discovered a way to manipulate time and escape certain death

JOE MARKHAM
He was a tough sailor. Then one day he bumped into a perfect stranger—and transformed into a whimpering underling.

DR. FREDERICK PONDER
If you needed someone to figure out why you thought you were going crazy, he was definitely your man.

THE INVISIBLE ONES
No one knew exactly who they were or how old they were, but in certain circumstances they held the power of life and death.

SURVIVORS
FROM
9000 B.C.

By
ROBERT MOORE WILLIAMS

ARMCHAIR FICTION
PO Box 4369, Medford, Oregon 97504

*For more information about Armchair Books and products, visit our
website at…*

www.armchairfiction.com

Or email us at…

armchairfiction@yahoo.com

CHAPTER ONE
Reunion with a Slave

"WHY don't you look who you're bumpin' into, Bud?" the big sailor truculently demanded.

Don King turned. He had been hurrying across the lobby of the building toward the bank of elevators and he had scarcely noticed that he had bumped into anyone. It was just one of those things that constantly occur in crowded New York, to be passed off with a terse, "Sorry." It meant nothing.

Don King started to murmur the usual polite phrase.

And then he knew it was going to happen again, that same horrible feeling that had come over him so often in the past. It was going to happen again!

What Don King had intended to say was choked off in his throat. He didn't say he was sorry. Instead his face grew red with violent anger, and in a snarling, savage voice, he rasped loudly:

"Down on your knees, you dog. Down, I say, before I have every bone in your body broken, before I have you beaten to a pulp and thrown from the cliffs into the sea. Down, you dirty dog, and beg for your worthless life. Down, I say!"

King was a husky chunk of a man, an inch under six feet, with the shoulders and hands of a prizefighter. Oddly, his youthful face was a mahogany brown, a trademark that could only have been left on him by the fierce tropical sun. In his gray eyes, fastened on the sailor, were two expressions, ruthless anger and terrible fear; two men seemed to look out of his eyes.

King was big. But the sailor was bigger. A good six foot three, and built in proportion, he towered over the smaller man. In a fair fight between the two, the wise money would have been on the sailor. Those long arms held a murderous strength, and the scar gouged down the left side of his face showed that he was no stranger to fighting.

He was big enough to tear King to pieces.

For an instant, he looked like he was going to do it. A terrible anger splashed itself over his face. He lifted his fists.

The two men had never seen each other before. They had bumped into each other as they hurried for the elevators. There was no justification for a fight. And yet, in the flash of an instant, over a trivial incident, they had squared off and were facing each other as if they intended to fly at each other's throat.

The lobby of the building was thronged. Startled passers-by hastily moved aside to gawk with incredulous eyes at the two men.

"Down," King hissed from between clenched teeth. "Down, you mangy cur, and beg for your worthless life!"

Muscles worked in the sailor's throat. A look of shocked surprise appeared on his face.

"Down!" King rasped.

A flowing tide of white was creeping over the sailor's face. There was a struggle going on within him. Fascinated, he stared at King, his features working. His hands clenched and unclenched.

An awed silence fell in the lobby.

"There's going to be a fight," somebody whispered.

"What's the matter with them?" a second person asked. "What are they mad about?"

"They bumped into each other," the explanation came.

"Bumped into each other! Gwan, they're not going to have a scrap over a little thing like that!"

"I saw it happen," the first person insisted. "That's all it was—they just bumped into each other."

"I don't give a darn if you did see it happen, there's more back of it than *that.*"

"Oh, golly, *look!*" somebody whispered excitedly.

The big sailor was groveling on the floor. Stretched full length in front of King, he was abjectly begging for his life.

"Master, Master," he was pleading. "Don't have poor Joe beaten. Joe didn't know what he was doing when he spoke to you like that, Joe didn't. Joe didn't mean anything. Please don't have poor Joe beaten, Master. He won't ever, ever, *ever* do it again. Please, Master, *please...*"

DON KING was looking down at him. His face was white with strain. He passed a hand in front of his eyes. Perspiration had appeared on his forehead. He pulled a handkerchief out of his coat pocket and wiped it away.

"Please, Master..." the big sailor begged.

A change had come over King. Only he knew how terrible a change it had been. The by-standers saw the terrible anger go out of his eyes, saw his whole body tremble as a convulsive shudder passed through it.

"Joe didn't mean anything," the sailor continued. "Joe didn't know what he was doing. Joe won't do it anymore."

"You poor devil," King said, his voice vibrant with compassion. "So it's got you too, has it?"

"Please don't have poor Joe beaten," the sailor answered.

"There now," King said. "You're not going to be beaten. Stand up, man. No one is going to harm you." He reached down and took the sailor by the arm, lifting him to his feet.

An awed, incredulous fear showed on the sailor's face. He trembled and tried to draw away from King.

"Don't be afraid," King said. "I'm sorry I spoke to you the way I did, but I—couldn't help myself. What's your name?"

"Joe Markham, Master."

King shook his head. "Don't call me master," he said.

"No, Master," the sailor answered.

King started to say something but changed his mind. The gawking curious crowd caught his eye. He suddenly took the sailor by the arm and led him, still trembling, to the elevator.

"Eleventh floor," King said to the operator.

The cage shot upward. Out of the corner of his eyes, King watched the sailor. The man was shaking like a leaf. When they got out of the elevator the sailor followed him, walking like a frightened dog following its owner. King mopped the sweat from his face and opened a door marked:

Dr. Frederick Ponder
Psychiatrist

Dr. Ponder was one of the most celebrated psychoanalysts in the world. Formerly a resident of Vienna—until political strife had driven him from his beloved city—he had been a student under the immortal Freud and he had been one of that group of gifted Viennese men who had contributed so much to the beginning science of the mind.

Dr. Ponder was in conference and King took a seat in his reception room.

"Sit down, Joe," he said sighing. "We'll have to wait a few minutes."

The suggestion seemed to horrify the sailor. "You want poor Joe to sit down with the Master?" he questioned.

King stared at him. Joe remained standing. King shook his head. He said nothing more. But fifteen minutes later, when the receptionist ushered him into the office of the psychiatrist, he was almost babbling when he spoke.

"Dr. Ponder, it's happened again. And this time it's worse than ever before. Is there anything under the sun that you can do to help me?"

PONDER was a little man. The heavy spectacles that he wore, his short but neatly clipped beard, and his heavy head of snow-white hair, made him look like an elderly but benevolent gnome. He blinked at the man who had entered, and then, recognizing his caller, was out of his chair in a single bound.

"Don. Don, my boy. It's glad I am to see you. You have been gone—let me see, it is over a year this last time, is it not? And where was it that you went? I cannot seem to remember."

"Morocco," King answered. "But let me tell you what just happened."

Tersely he outlined the events that had taken place in the lobby. Ponder, his eyes blinking behind the thick spectacles that he wore, sat back in his chair and listened, a thoughtful, intensely worried expression on his face.

"This man—this sailor—did you ever see him before?" he questioned.

"Never in my life," King answered. "When I bumped into him, I started to say I was sorry and keep moving. But something seemed to grab me. Suddenly I wasn't Don King any longer. I was somebody else. This sailor had offended me and I was terribly angry at him. It seemed to me that I had the power of life and death over him, that I could have him beaten, that I could have him killed. I was going to have him killed, if he didn't get down on his knees and beg for his life.

"I was on my way to see you at the time. But the strangest part, Doctor, was that the sailor seemed to recognize me. He called me master. He begged for his life. Doctor..." King asked, horror and bewilderment in his voice. "Who am I? What on earth is the matter with me? Why should all these things happen to me?"

The psychoanalyst gazed thoughtfully at the man seated across the desk from him. He said nothing. Instead he went to a card file in a corner of the room and took a bulky manila folder from it. He began to rifle through the sheets of paper it contained.

"Six years ago," he said, "when you were twenty and just after you had finished college, your left arm went dead."

"It didn't go dead," King remonstrated. "I couldn't move it. But the oddest part was that I didn't seem to have an arm. And when it did move, it seemed to move of its own accord. I couldn't control it. It would suddenly jump up, the fingers would clench, and it would seem to try to hit somebody—somebody who wasn't present."

Ponder nodded. "The condition lasted four days and then went away as suddenly as it had appeared. That was the first sign of abnormality. The second—"

Sweating, Don King listened as the psychoanalyst went over all of the terrible things that had happened. How vividly King remembered them! Six years ago it had started, with his left arm going bad. After that—

It was just after he had finished college. He was home with his parents. One morning he had awakened to find himself miles from his home, clad only in pajamas, his feet cut and bleeding, with no knowledge of how he had got there. He had walked in his sleep. The police had brought the dazed youth home.

Next, one of his legs had gone dead. It had lost all feeling. Then it had seemed to develop a will of its own and had tried to walk away with him!

THEN the nightmares had come. Don King shuddered when he remembered them. They had been horrible. In them he had been an entirely different person. This person had inflicted terrible tortures on helpless slaves, he had had their eyes pierced with needles, molten lead poured in their ears.

Next had come the wanderlust, an uncontrollable urge to visit far-away countries. King had fought it, without success. One morning he had found himself signed on a tramp steamer bound for Central America. Odder still, he had jumped ship in Yucatan, and had spent a year exploring the Mayan ruins in that country. He was looking for something there, *but he did not know what he was looking for!* Something. He hadn't found it.

After that, the same uncontrollable urge had taken him to the Basque country in northern Spain. Again he did not know what he was looking for. He had wandered through the mountains inhabited by that curious people of whose origin science knows nothing. He had learned the Basque language, in itself an extraordinary achievement, for the Basque tongue is different from all other known languages. But King had picked it up easily.

He had returned to America, and again the wanderlust had struck him. This time it had taken him to Egypt. He had wanted to see the Grand Pyramid of Giza, that strange construction erected in the land of Egypt before the dawn of trustworthy history. Seeing that pyramid, he was conscious only of extreme regret. Somehow it was different from what he had expected it to be. He had spent over a year in the land of the Pharaohs, wandering up and down the valley of the Nile, searching—for something.

From there, the mad wanderlust that controlled him had taken him to Morocco, back into the Atlas Mountains, over the sands of the Sahara. He did not know what he expected to find there. Whatever it was, he had not found it.

If he could only know what he was searching for! If he could only know why he had gone to Yucatan, to the Basque country, to Egypt, to Morocco!

If he could only know why he had snarled so savagely at the sailor! And why the sailor had dropped to the floor in front of him!

"Do I have a split personality, Doctor?" King asked. "Am I another Dr. Jekyll and Mr. Hyde?"

The psychoanalyst shook his head.

"I think not, Don. No, there is more here than a split personality. It is, I think, one of the strangest cases in medical history."

"But is there any way to cure me? Is there anything I can do? Every time somebody bumps into me, I can't call them a mangy dog and order them to get down on their knees and beg for their life. Is there any way to get rid of this madness that obsesses me?"

Slowly Dr. Ponder shook his head.

"You are looking for something, Don. What it is neither you nor I nor anyone else knows. But when you find it, you will also find yourself."

"But what am I looking for?" King asked. "You've been treating me ever since my arm went dead six years ago. You have dug into my mind so deeply that you know more about me than I know about myself. Can you tell me what I am seeking?"

"I think I can," the psychoanalyst answered. "But you must remember that my answer is nothing more than a guess, with no scientific backing."

"What is it?" King asked eagerly.

"Yourself," Ponder answered.

"Myself?" King echoed.

"Your *other* self," the doctor said.

HE got out of his chair and began to walk up and down the room, muttering strange oaths in his own language.

"I cannot be certain that I am right, Don," he said finally. "Ach, who knows what is true and what is untrue... The human mind, a great mystery it is. How does the mind work? Nobody knows definitely. Not even the great Freud could be sure. What is the mind? Again, there is no answer. But Don, the possibility there is—just a bare possibility it is—that you are the reincarnation of somebody else."

"Reincarnation!" King blurted out. "But—but that's impossible."

"Who knows what is impossible and what is not? Millions of people believe in reincarnation. It is just possible that you are the reincarnation of someone who lived a long time ago, some very savage, very cruel person. That would explain why you were going to have the sailor whipped."

"But this wanderlust," King protested. "How do you explain that?"

"I can't," the psychoanalyst answered. "I can't explain anything. All I can do is guess. But there is an explanation, somewhere. Never doubt that there is an explanation. You went to Yucatan, to Egypt, to Morocco, to the Basque country. Somewhere there is a thread that will give a complete explanation of why you went to these places, just as somewhere there is an explanation of everything that has happened to you."

He paused and looked at the man sitting in the chair in his office. There was a haunted, horror-stricken expression on King's face.

"Don, you must be very careful," he said. "For unless I miss my guess, this wanderlust will come to you again. Sooner or later it will take you to the place you are seeking. You will face great danger, Don, terrible danger. What this danger will be I cannot tell you. I do not know. But it is ahead of you."

There was pity in the doctor's voice. Pity and awe. Pity for the man whom he could not help. Awe, because he sensed that through this man there flowed the thread of a tremendous mystery.

Don King rose to his feet.

"Is this all you can tell me?" he asked.

Ponder gravely nodded.

"I wish it could be more, Don. But nobody knows. The science of the mind is too young. But be on the look-out. When this other person, of whom you are the reincarnation, seizes control of you, fight. You can conquer him, you can overcome him. But I doubt if you will be able to overcome the wanderlust. When it calls, you will have to answer. But beware of where it leads you, for, unless I miss my guess, it will lead you face to face with death itself."

"Thanks for the warning," said King huskily. "I'll try to be prepared."

HE walked out of the office. In the reception room, Joe Markham rose hastily to his feet.

"Will you return home now, Master?" the sailor said.

King was suddenly trembling. Home! Master! The wanderlust was coming over him again. Something, somewhere on the face of the earth, was pulling him. But this time it was telling him to go with this sailor, that Joe Markham was a guide who would take him to the unknown place he was seeking...

He saw, also, the submissive manner of the man. The sailor was actually cowering before him. King saw what it meant. If he was the reincarnation of some person dead for uncounted centuries, then this sailor might also be a reincarnation—*of his slave!* There seemingly could be no other meaning. The humble, cowering attitude of the man, was that of a slave...

The realization shocked King to the bottom of his soul.

He did not want a slave. Slavery belonged back in the hideous past of the race. But whether he wanted one or not, he had him.

"Joe—" King whispered. "You're not a slave. Do you understand? You're not a slave."

Doubt showed on the weather-beaten face.

"I do not understand, Master," the answer came.

King groaned.

"We'll settle this later, Joe," he said. "And now there is one question I want to ask you?"

"Yes, Master."

"Can you take me home?"

The sailor seemed to act like a man in a trance. Doubt and uncertainty showed on his face.

"I—I think so, Master," he said hesitantly. "It is far away, but I seem to know how to go. We will need to take passage on a ship, Master, but I think I know what ship we will go on. Yes. I think I can take the master home."

"Good," said King grimly. Subdued elation surged through his heart. At long last he might find out who he was. At last he might know what he had sought in the strangest places of the Earth!

But mindful of the doctor's warning, he went first to a sporting goods store and purchased guns.

CHAPTER TWO
Mystery in the Sea

"THERE'S something splashing in the sea astern of us," the man at the wheel nervously called out.

Don King and Joe Markham were sprawled on the amidship hatch, smoking a final cigarette before turning in for the night. They had taken passage on a small, English-owned sailing ship. The sailor, walking like a man in a trance, had taken Don King to this ship. King had been tremendously surprised to learn that sailing ships were still in use. But the sailor had been certain that this was the vessel he was seeking.

"This is the ship, Boss," he had said. "It will take us near home."

The vessel, loaded with lumber, was bound for the Azores.

Now it had been four days caught in that great windless area that lies near the Azores. The night was moonless and dark and the ship was wallowing in a slick, silent sea. The sails hung lifelessly from the yardarms overhead. There was no wind. Not even the trace of a breeze stirred the rigging.

In that silent sea something was splashing.

King raised himself on one elbow and listened. He could hear the sound plainly. Something was raising a tremendous hubbub in the water. Sharp cracks, like huge fins beating the surface, came through the night.

"Do you suppose it is a school of porpoises?" he asked.

"I don't know, Boss," Joe Markham answered. "But I never heard porpoises make that much noise."

In the two weeks that had passed since they took passage on this vessel, King had succeeded in overcoming much of the sailor's abject fear of him.

Between the two men a warm friendship had sprung up. They had a common bond. Under King's questioning, Markham had admitted that he, too, had been afflicted just as King had been. He had suffered from the loss of the use of his arms and legs and the same resistless wanderlust that drove King had also driven Markham, with the result that he had turned to the sea. There was no doubt in either of their minds that they had at some remote time been master and slave. Nor did they doubt that their destiny—whatever it was—was somehow the same.

But was there a connection between the strange fate that ruled them and this sudden splashing in the sea astern of the ship?

They arose and walked to the stern of the vessel. The helmsman was peering into the darkness behind them.

"What do you think it is?" King inquired.

"Might be a killer whale," he answered. "Maybe a couple of killers in a fight."

"Did you ever hear whales make that much noise?"

"No," the helmsman slowly answered. "I never did."

The splashing increased in volume.

"It's following us," the helmsman said nervously. "I've been hearing it for maybe half an hour. At first it was far away. But now it's coming a lot closer."

King and Markham leaned over the rail, trying to locate the source of the sound. Strain their eyes as they might, they could see nothing.

"I don't like it," Markham muttered. "Do you think it's got anything to do with—us?"

King shook his head. A subtle tension was beginning to creep over him. An eerie chill moved up and down his spine. In the darkness behind the ship the splashing grew louder. There was no longer any doubt but that something was following the ship. But what was it? King slipped his hand inside the leather jacket he was wearing, felt of the heavy automatic pistol snuggled in the shoulder holster. The feel of the gun was slightly reassuring.

BY now the watch was clustering along the rail, listening to the sullen splashing sounds. The crew of the ship was mostly made up of boys between the ages of sixteen and eighteen, serving an apprenticeship in sail under seasoned officers. Normally they were as talkative as magpies. But now they were silent.

The helmsman sent one of them below to awaken the captain. Somebody must have awakened the sleeping crew, for they came piling on deck and joined their comrades at the rail, nor did the captain send them below.

The threshing noises seemed to lessen.

"It's going away," someone muttered thankfully. The puzzled crew began to relax. Even though they were youngsters, all of them had already absorbed the superstitions of the sea. The heavy, sullen splashes coming closer and closer to the ship had roused their fears of the supernatural. Scratch the surface of any seaman and there will be found, if not a belief in, at least a terribly pathetic fear of the monsters of the sea.

Had a sea monster been chasing them? King wondered.

"It's gone," one of the crew whispered. "It's gone away. What do you think it was?" he asked one of his comrades.

Before the lad had time to answer everyone on the ship knew that it hadn't gone away.

A cry came echoing across the water, a shrill sharp wail that set Don King's teeth on edge. Automatically his hand dived under his jacket for the pistol holstered there. Out of the corner of his eyes he saw Markham jerk nervously as the cry came.

The cry was shrill and blatant. It roared across the sea in two brazen notes. It died in a gulping murmur.

By no stretch of the imagination could that cry have come from any creature known to inhabit the ocean. The splashes might conceivably have been caused by a school of whales playing on the surface. But no whale could have uttered that cry.

"The sea demon!" the old helmsman gasped.

"Nonsense!" the captain said sharply. But there was no conviction in his voice.

The splashing sounds came again, louder now, closer.

Suddenly an apprentice yelled.

"Something black's coming toward us!"

King saw a dark object, like the conning tower of a submarine, slithering through the water toward them.

The captain, apparently thinking it was a submarine, roared, "Sub ahoy!"

There was no answer.

"Sheer off!" the captain shouted. "You damned fools, you'll run us down. Show a light!" he bellowed at the crew.

Someone grabbed a lantern and swung it back and forth. The light only seemed to make the thing come faster. It was plainly visible now, splashing through the waves toward them. And there was no mistaking its intention—it was after the ship!

KING found himself with the pistol in his hand, nervously waiting—for what?

"Down with the helm!" the captain ordered, springing to the wheel to assist the helmsman.

The ship, deep in water, was sluggish. She had no engine. On top of that, there was no wind. The ship, lacking steerageway, refused to respond to the helm. They couldn't dodge the thing that was coming toward them, and with no wind, they certainly couldn't out run it.

"What do you think it is, Boss?" Markham gasped.

"We'll soon know, Joe," King answered.

Then the cry came again. Shrill and sharp it daggered through the night. This time there was a gloating, excited note in it—the same note that sounds in the bugling of the running hound hot on the scent of fleeing prey.

Even more incredible than the cry itself, was the fact that it seemed to form words.

"Kra-*kor!* Kra-*kor!*"

King gasped in blank bewilderment. The wailing cry that came through the night formed words! Rather, it formed a single word, twice repeated.

But more incredible than that was the fact that he understood the word! Vaguely, dimly, and yet unmistakably, he knew what that single word meant!

Then the black monstrosity out of the ocean night was on them.

King saw something black and snakelike come up over the stern of the ship. It tapered to a pointed end and he had the fleeting impression that a rope was being thrown aboard. Instantly he knew it was not a rope. It wrapped its snaky length around the man at the wheel, lifted him ten feet into the air, and while it jerked him overboard, *literally squeezed him into two pieces.* His scream of mad fright and madder pain choked off in a horrid gurgle.

Every man on board the ship saw death come to the helmsman. Like a frozen blanket, silence fell. It was broken only by the labored breathing of horribly frightened men and the splashing sounds coming from the monster in the sea.

The mad scream of an apprentice broke the silence. Instantly there was pandemonium on the ship as the crew fled forward.

"What'll we do now, Boss?" Joe Markham husked.

"Fight!" King grimly answered. "You've got a gun. Use it."

He leaped to the rail. A black mass was moving through the water approaching the side of the ship. The pistol jerked in his hand as he pressed the trigger. He fired as fast as he could work the weapon. Beside him, Markham, leaning over the rail, was also firing.

A sullen clanging came from the monster. It seemed not to feel the heavy slugs smashing into it. Its pace did not slacken.

"We're not doing any damage," Markham yelled.

"I was afraid of that!" King groaned. "Our pistols aren't heavy enough."

Forward he caught a glimpse of the crew. They were trying to lower a lifeboat, but in their panic they had so tangled the rigging that the boat could not be dropped.

He saw another of the ropes come shooting up out of the water. He knew what they were. They weren't ropes. They were *tentacles!*

The captain seized an ax. With it he slashed viciously at the tentacle. It was the brave act of a courageous man. It was also his last act. Two of the tentacles seized him. His screams retched through the air as the tentacles, one grasping him around the feet and the other around the body, pulled him to pieces.

King was sick. Before his eyes two good men had died in terrible agony.

"Look out, Boss!" he heard Joe Markham shriek.

SIMULTANEOUSLY he was knocked off his feet. As he hit the deck, he caught a glimpse of a tentacle waving in the air above him. It was reaching toward him, fingering in every direction. He rolled, and it followed him like a snake.

"Boss! Watch out!" Markham screamed.

King saw the tentacle diving forward him.

Simultaneously Markham fired at it. The slug smashed into the ropy length. About three feet of it suddenly went limp. Markham's bullet had damaged it. It hung uncertainly in the air for a second and then was jerked back overboard.

"Thanks, Joe," King gasped, getting to his feet. "You saved my life."

"We better get forward," the sailor answered, "before one of those tentacles tears us in two."

"That's good advice," King answered. He and the sailor started to run forward, but as they did so, the ship listed violently, throwing both of them to their knees. King's first thought was that a sudden squall had struck them, forcing the ship to heel over.

With wind to fill the sails they could outrun the monster ranging alongside. Wind! A squall!

Grabbing a rope, King pulled himself to his feet. The ship heeled over again, the whole heavily laden vessel rocking to and fro as if it were caught in a mighty gale. A splintering crash sounded. Then King saw why the ship was heeling over.

It wasn't because of a wind. The sea was still flat and greasy. There was no sudden squall that had struck them. The monster had come alongside and was trying to climb aboard. Its weight was causing the ship to heel over so violently!

The vessel, though small in comparison with an ocean liner, was huge when compared to any creature known to inhabit the sea. Yet the thing climbing aboard weighed enough to make the whole ship list heavily.

Again the cry roared out. "Kra-*kor*. Kra-*kor*..."

King got the impression that it waited for an answer.

And from far distance an answer came! A shrill, clean, note of a horn raced across the waters.

"Kra-*kor!*"

Again the horn note sounded. It was closer this time.

"There are two of them!" Joe Markham gasped. "They're calling to each other. Boss, what are we going to do now?"

"Go below," King answered. "If we stay up here one of those tentacles—"

The words were choked off in his throat. As he started down the companionway one of the tentacles struck him heavily. It was like the blow of a mighty fist. Stars splashed before King's eyes. The blow knocked him off balance. He fell down the companionway, struck with a sickening crash at the bottom. The stars flashing before his eyes dissolved into utter blackness.

He vaguely knew the fall had knocked him out. As consciousness faded, he dimly heard, rising above the crashing of the monster climbing aboard the vessel, the horn blowing in the distance.

CHAPTER THREE
The Unknown Island

KING awakened to find the frightened face of Joe Markham bending over him. His head was throbbing with a splitting ache and as he tried to get to his feet, his whole skull threatened to explode. He fell back.

He was lying on the bunk in his own cabin. Apparently the sailor had brought him there. Light was coming in through the portholes.

The ship was silent, as though at anchor. When under sail the vessel creaked and groaned. But now she was silent.

King, his mind reverting to the incredible creature that had attacked them, listened again for that weird cry that had come hurtling through the night. He did not hear it.

"What happened, Joe?" he whispered. "Where are we?"

"Boss," the sailor answered huskily. "We're *there.*"

"There? What do you mean?"

"We've found the place we've both been trying to find," Markham whispered, his scarred face tense with fear. "The place you looked for in Egypt, and Spain, and Central America, and didn't find. We're *there,* Boss."

An electric thrill shot through King. The unknown, hidden place that he sought—he had found it!

"Where is it? Where are we?" he demanded eagerly.

The sailor somberly shook his head. "It's an island. But where it is I don't know. The ship was towed to it, but I didn't dare go up on top to see where we were being taken.

I looked through the portholes as we came in. We were brought into a big hole in a cliff. Right now we're floating in a pool in some kind of an underground cavern."

An island, King thought. It must be somewhere near the Azores. The place toward which the wanderlust had driven him was out in the Atlantic Ocean! It wasn't in Spain, or Egypt, or Central America. It was an island in the sea.

"What happened after I got knocked out?" he questioned. "What about the monster that was attacking us?"

A superstitious tremor passed over the sailor's face.

"It wrapped its tentacles around the ship and held us. It didn't really try to come aboard. It just grabbed us and held on tight. And all the time it kept screaming and that horn kept answering it, coming closer and closer."

"Then what?" King questioned.

"Boss," the sailor answered huskily. "There was somebody or something in a boat. *It* talked to whatever was in the boat."

"What do you mean by *it?*"

Markham shivered.

"The monster. It talked to whoever was in the boat. It shrilled and whistled and screamed and somebody in the boat told it what to do. Anyhow it jerked all the sails off the ship. Then it tore down the masts. It snapped them into pieces, Boss, just like you or I would break a match in our fingers. Then it began to tow the ship.

"Boss, I tell you it took us through the water faster than any ship I was ever in before. All the time, the boat stayed with us, its horn squawking like the devil himself. It brought us here to this cavern. We've been here maybe half an hour. The monster may still have hold of the ship, for all I know. I haven't gone outside to see."

KING lay still, trying to understand what Markham had told him. His head was beginning to clear. The ache was subsiding. His strength was slowly coming back.

"What happened to the crew?" he asked.

"They went overboard," Markham gloomily answered. "Some of them may be hiding in the hold. I don't know. But most of them went overboard. That thing scared them so badly they jumped in the sea. They're fish food by now."

King winced at the thought of the crew diving into the sea. Many of them couldn't swim at all and none of them could swim well enough to reach land.

"Somebody or something will get paid off for what happened to the crew," he said bitterly. He got to his feet, walked across the cabin and opened his bags. Methodically he reloaded his pistol and filled his pockets with cartridges.

"You do the same," he ordered Markham. "Sooner or later, we'll need these guns."

The sailor was looking through the porthole.

"I think it will be sooner, Boss," he said, turning to King. "There's a boat coming to see about us."

King leaped to the port. He was just in time to see a large barge vanish around the stern of the ship. The barge looked like the pictures he had seen of Roman and Greek galleys. It had neither sails nor engines. *It was propelled by oars!*

The barge grated against the side of the ship. There was a loud *thump* as of a gangplank being thrown aboard. A harsh voice rasped an order. Feet clumped on the deck overhead.

"Keep your gun out of sight," said King. "We're going up to meet our fate."

With King leading the way and Markham following right behind him, they climbed the steps to the deck.

Emerging, King caught a glimpse of a huge cavern. It was a tremendous thing, stretching dimly away into the distance farther than he could see. A series of round holes cut in the roof overhead shed a misty golden illumination over the scene. The ship was lying in a large pool. To one side was what looked like a deserted city. Connecting the pool in which the ship was lying and the city was a canal. There seemed to be many of the canals and the impression King got in a single hasty glance was that this place much resembled the city of Venice, except that it was underground.

King only had time for a hasty glance. He found himself face to face with a squad of soldiers.

They were not clad as were the soldiers of the United States army, in brown khaki. Nor did they wear tin hats and carry rifles. They were dressed in chain armor, helmeted like knights, and they carried round shields and long lances.

King stared at them in amazement. Their armor and their weapons belonged to a day that was hundreds—if not thousands—of years past!

They in turn gaped at him. But only for an instant. Then their leader recovered from his astonishment and rasped an order. King found himself facing a row of sharp lance points.

"Stand aside, Boss," he heard Markham whisper from behind him. "We'll mow these rats down. If they think that tin armor they're wearing will stop a slug from a .45

they've got another think coming. Get out of the way, Boss, and we'll let 'em have it."

"No!" King hissed. "Keep your gun out of sight. Before we do any shooting, there're lot of things we need to know."

The officer in charge of the squad hastily called back to the barge, apparently for further orders.

"Bring them before me," a voice said.

THE words were not in English but Don King understood them. At the moment, he was not greatly surprised to discover that he had understood. The language in which the command had been couched was very similar to Basque. There were differences but they were slight. He understood quite clearly. In the press of circumstances he did not remember that the Basque language is not definitely related to any known language on earth today, although efforts have been made to link it both with Sanskrit and the tongues spoken by various North American Indian tribes.

Don King was thinking: here is where I find out what is wrong with me. Here is where I find an explanation for the numbness that has occasionally struck my arms and legs. Here I will find the secret of my wanderlust. Only he knew how desperately important the solution of the mystery was to him. Certainly his sanity and very probably his life depended on his finding the solution. But he had not forgotten the warning of Dr. Ponder:

"Be very careful, Don. When you find what you seek, you will also find great danger."

He was conscious of a surge of elation as the squad of soldiers formed a guard around them and marched them, King leading, down the gangplank and on to the barge.

Here, on this barge, he would find the solution to the mystery.

At the stern of the barge, under a canopy, was a wooden chair that evidently served as a throne. This was a king's barge then. Seated on the steps below the throne was a girl. She shot a startled glance at King as he approached. Her gaze came back to him and stayed there. There was shocked, bewildered fear on her face.

King scarcely saw the girl. As soon as he came before the throne, he stopped short.

Seated on the throne was a man. Wearing a barbaric headdress, a small double-bladed ax in his hands that was evidently his scepter, the man glanced down at the captives being brought before him. There was an indolent sneer on his face. And something of curiosity, but the sneer was more pronounced.

King was stricken speechless. He did not know exactly what he had expected to find on this barge, but he thought that it could be just about anything—*anything but this.*

The man on the throne was King's exact double! The two men could not have resembled each other any more if they had been twin brothers. The strong jaw, the high forehead, the firm but delicate nose. Except for the sneer, they were exactly the same. The only difference was the sneer and the fact that King's face was tanned a mahogany brown in contrast to the face of the ruler, which was a pasty white.

"Down on your knees, you dog," the ruler rasped. "Don't you have any manner or are you attempting to defy Dor Diavo? Down on your knees—"

KING did not move. He couldn't have moved if he had wanted to. Surprise held him motionless. Now he understood what the psychiatrist had meant when he had said, "You will meet yourself."

King was either meeting himself face to face or he was meeting a man who was his exact double.

The ruler stopped. He stared at King, for the first time noticing how much this prisoner resembled him.

The officer of the guard, interpreting his ruler's orders, stepped forward and struck King heavily on the shoulder, forcing him to the floor. Snarling, he leaped to his feet.

"Tell your men to keep their hands off of me—" he began. Then he saw the man on the throne was no longer looking at him. The ruler was looking at Joe Markham. The sneer on his face had turned to fear. He was cowering back on his throne.

"I had you beaten and thrown from the cliffs into the sea," he was whispering. "You're dead. You can't be alive. Like a clumsy fool, you stumbled into me. I had you killed. Go away..."

The ruler's face was gray with rising fear. He thought he was looking at a ghost, risen from the grave to haunt him.

King's mind was racing. He remembered how he and Joe Markham had bumped into each other, and he remembered the violent rage that had suddenly possessed him, the words that had leaped unbidden from his savagely snarling lips.

"Down on your knees, you dog, and beg for your worthless life. Down on your knees, I say, before I have every bone in your body broken, before I have you beaten to a pulp and thrown into the sea."

King, in the lobby of a building in New York City, had been repeating the words of the ruler of this incredible island here in the Atlantic Ocean. Here a slave had bumped into the ruler, into Dor Diavo. And Dor Diavo had snarled at him.

In New York City almost the same situation had existed. King's lips had repeated Dor Diavo's words. While that terrible spell had held him, he had snarled at Joe Markham just as Dor Diavo had snarled at his slave. Dor Diavo had put the slave to death. But now the reincarnation of that slave had come before him. Joe Markham was the reincarnation of the slave who had been beaten to death.

And Don King was the reincarnation of this ruler who sat on the throne here in this unknown Atlantic Island! Their complete resemblance to each other, King's strange wanderlust, his periodic loss of control of certain parts of his body, everything pointed to one conclusion and one conclusion only—Don King was the reincarnation of Dor Diavo.

One question was thundering like an echo in King's mind. How could he be the reincarnation of a man who was still alive? Dor Diavo was very much alive. King was alive. What mad mystery was hidden behind this incredible fact?

"Where did you come from?" the ruler quavered, looking at Markham.

THE sailor was too stunned to make an attempt to answer. Hate was digging grooves in his face. His eyes had narrowed. His great hands were balled into fists. He had dropped into a crouch and—poised on his toes— looked like he was ready to leap at the ruler. All his actions showed that at first sight he instinctively hated the man who sat on the throne above him, the man who had ordered him beaten and thrown into the sea in a previous incarnation.

"Hold it, Joe," King hissed, speaking in English. "Don't jump him. You'll only get yourself killed."

The sailor looked at King. A little of the hate disappeared from his face. He looked hopelessly bewildered. But he dropped his arms.

"If it pleases Your Majesty," the officer of the squad of soldiers answered in a formal sounding tone. "They were both on board this strange ship that we captured last night. But we don't know from whence they came. When we discovered them, we brought them immediately into your presence, knowing that your great wisdom would enable you to deal with them."

The ruler regained a little of his shattered composure.

"Where did you come from?" he again demanded.

"From America," Don King answered.

"America? I've never heard of the place. Is it, perchance, one of the lands beyond the Middle Sea?".

It was King's turn to gasp. "It lies to the west," he tried to explain. "It is composed of two great continents, North and South America, which stretch from pole to pole."

"Mayan!" Dor Diavo gasped. "You came from Mayan? Tell me: What happened to our colonies there? Many times I have wanted to know."

"Colonies?" King echoed. "I don't know what you mean. Great Britain, the Netherlands, and France have small colonies in the Americas, but they amount to very little. The two great continents are inhabited by free and independent peoples."

His reply seemed to astonish the ruler. But Dor Diavo did not question him further. Instead he abruptly changed the subject.

"How does it happen," he queried, "that you so much resemble me, man from America?"

"Although I don't understand it myself," King answered steadily, "I think the only possible explanation is that I am a reincarnation of you."

The words came easily to his lips, but the instant they were uttered he sensed that he had said the wrong thing. Dor Diavo's face seemed to freeze. A malevolent gleam leaped into his eyes. Silence fell.

In that sudden stillness King could hear the harsh breathing of their guards. He saw the face of the officer. There was startled fright in it. And the girl who during this talk had remained seated below the throne looking wonderingly at King, suddenly rose to her feet. For an instant she stared at King, inexplicable hope gleaming in her eyes. Tremulously she smiled at him.

"He who comes again," she whispered.

The smile was wiped off her face in a second when Dor Diavo rasped in angry tones.

"Seize them! Bind, gag, and blindfold them."

King's hand dived for his gun. Before these devils threw him into some stinking prison hole, they would find they had a fight on their hands. His fingers closed around the butt of the pistol. Simultaneously one of the guards struck him on the head with the flat side of a lance. A ball of light exploded before his eyes. He felt himself falling.

Grimly he fought back to his feet, all the time trying to draw the gun. But before he could get the weapon drawn, a wave of bodies bore him to the floor. He fought like a tiger, but in spite of all he could do, he found his arms pinioned behind him. Loops of cord slid over his wrists. A fold of cloth was thrust into his mouth, another clapped over his eyes.

"Imprison them," he heard Dor Diavo order.

"Golly, Boss," Joe Markham choked through his own gag. "What did we do wrong?"

CHAPTER FOUR
In Prison

"THIS is the explanation," the pale girl said. She had come to them secretly in the night, slipping past the guards who kept constant watch in the corridor outside. "You are unquestionably the reincarnation of Dor Diavo. You have grown up in different countries, under different conditions, so that you think differently, but essentially you are the same man. We know that this sometimes happens. Our wise men have kept records for thousands of years, and have discovered many instances of a man being born again.

"It has happened to you. You not only look like Dor Diavo. You *are* Dor Diavo, who has come again to life. That is why you are in great danger. You look too much like the ruler. You might kill him, and take his place, and no one would ever know the difference. You might declare he is an usurper, and urge the people to rise against him. Many would follow you, for Dor Diavo has not been a gentle ruler."

"You don't have to evade the issue," King interrupted. "What is he going to do to me?"

"I—" the girl faltered.

"Out with it," said King.

"I don't want to tell you."

"I can stand it," the American answered. "I understand that I am a menace to the ruler. What is he going to do about it?"

"He will have you…killed." the pale girl replied.

King said nothing. His mouth set in a grim harsh line.

"It seems I am two men," he finally answered. "So one of us must die. I can understand that. But what I can't understand is how I am the reincarnation of a *living* man. It is normally a question of heredity. What reincarnation means is that a person alive today is a throwback to some remote ancestor who lived thousands of years ago. Separation in time is involved. But Dor Diavo and I are alive at the same time. He cannot possibly be one of my ancestors, nor is it likely that we have a common ancestor. We are about the same age and were born about the same time—"

"But you aren't the same age," the girl protested. "Don't you understand? I thought everything had been explained. Dor Diavo and you were not born at about the same time. He was born at least eleven thousand years before you were!"

"What?" the word leaped from King's lips. "But that's impossible..." he flatly stated. "You're talking nonsense!"

The girl faced him.

"Don't you understand?" she pleaded. "Dor Diavo—myself—all of us, this whole group belongs to the past. We belong to a period that your world has probably forgotten. *We were transported in time.* Dor Diavo did it. When he saw the catastrophe that was threatening us, he knew the only way to escape was to move forward in time. He and the wise men, brought us out of the past."

KING sat down heavily on the stone bench that was all the furniture in the cell. His mind reeled under the meaning of what the girl had just told him. Dor Diavo and his people, possibly this strange island in the Atlantic, had been transported in time.

148

In a flash he saw that this explained how he could be the reincarnation of the ruler. Time travel. Two men born eleven thousands years apart, one the reincarnation of the other, had met face to face because one of them had traveled in time.

It was also the explanation for the strange garb of the soldiers, for the armour they wore and the weapons they used, for the ruler's barge driven by oars.

"Where—what country—what time—did you come from?" he faltered.

"From Atlantis..." the girl answered. "We are the remnant of the Atlantans who escaped the catastrophe that overwhelmed our island thousands of years ago."

Atlantis! The word was a bell ringing in King's mind. Atlantis, the lost land of legend that Plato had said once existed beyond the Pillars of Hercules. Atlantis, where civilization had first flowered in the long gone past of Earth's hidden history. Persistent theories had credited the Atlantans with establishing colonies in Egypt and in Central America, colonies that had eventually almost forgotten the source from which they sprang after the motherland was destroyed.

And Dor Diavo had eagerly inquired, "What of our colonies in Mayan?" The ruler knew that those colonies had once existed and he had wondered what had happened to them.

"Then that explains my wanderlust," King whispered. "Dor Diavo wondered what had happened to the colonies of Atlantis. He wanted to revisit them, but for some reason he didn't. His impulse to visit them was transmitted to me in the form of a strange urge to visit these lands.

"That's what I was looking for in Central America and in Egypt! The lost colonies of my people. Probably the

Basques were another colony, which explains why I picked up their language so easily. And there must have been another colony in what is now the Sahara Desert. That's what I am—an Atlantan! I was born in America but some of my ancestors, thousands of years ago, must have come from Atlantis!"

He had risen to his feet and was pacing the floor. The whole incredible picture was clear at last. Now he knew who he was, now he knew the maddening secret of his own identity. He was the far-removed descendant of some Atlantan. Somewhere in the dead past of Atlantis he and Dor Diavo had had a common ancestor.

"How long has it been since you came out of time?" he questioned.

"Six years," the girl replied.

Even the time checked. The date when King had first lost control of his arm checked with Dor Diavo's first appearance in the present.

"Tell me about the people here on this island," King said. "How many are there? Tell me about Atlantis."

"Not counting slaves, there are about six hundred of us, which was all Dor Diavo chose to bring through time. The others he left to perish in the catastrophe that was to follow. But how can I tell you about Atlantis? Surely the whole world knows the glories of Atlantis!"

"I'm afraid the world has forgotten," King answered.

UNDER his questioning, she retold the story of that land where civilization had first come to flower. It had begun so far back in the past that even she, who had come across eleven thousand years of time, could not tell when it started.

The girl talked hurriedly, in a voice little above a whisper, occasionally darting nervous glances back over her shoulder at the door. King had been so fascinated by the story she was telling that he had completely forgotten the danger that surrounded them. Her glances reminded him of it.

It was then that he began to wonder how she had evaded the guards posted at the end of the corridor outside the prison cell. The guards had not brought her to the doorway. She had opened the door herself, cautiously lifting the heavy bar and slipping quickly through.

Had she bribed the jail keepers he wondered?

Why had she come in the first place? He hadn't asked her that. All he knew about her was that she had been seated on the steps below Dor Diavo's throne on the barge. He had scarcely noticed her there, except that she had smiled at him.

Who was she? Where did she fit into the picture? And most of all why should he be so drawn to her?

"I am Sonthia," she said, when he questioned her. "And I came to you for help, Don King."

King smiled wryly.

"You came to a poor place. Joe and I need help ourselves."

"You sure said a mouthful there, Boss," Markham said, speaking for the first time.

"We will help each other," the girl spoke quickly.

"What can I do?" King asked.

"You can be our ruler, Don King. Plans have already been made. Dor Diavo is in his chambers, sleeping. He will awaken to find himself a captive. You will take his place. You look exactly like him. No one will ever question that the reincarnation of Dor Diavo rules instead of him."

King was taken aback. "But—"

"You need have no fears, Don King," Sonthia said. "Through our crafts, we knew that you existed in this new time. We knew eventually you would come here. A few of us, who have reason to hate Dor Diavo, prepared everything for the day when you would come. And he played neatly into our hands. He had you brought here to this secret cell. No one has seen you, other than the squad of guards. No one will ever know that you have taken Dor Diavo's place. We will have a new ruler—"

King stared at her. Was she telling the truth? Or was this some trap? After all, what did he know about her? Perhaps she was trying to trick him.

"Don't you understand, Don King?" she burst out. "I hate Dor Diavo. He brought me here to this time with him, because he wanted me for his plaything. But my parents, my brothers and sisters, my friends, he left back in the old time, to perish in the terrible catastrophe that he knew was coming. Everyone that I loved, he killed. Me, he kept alive. That is why I hate him, Don King. That is why you must help not only me but all of us.

"Dor Diavo is cruel and ruthless. All whom he brought to this new time he holds as slaves. We are not strong enough to overthrow him by force. He is too powerful and too cunning for us. If we revolted, he would have us beaten and thrown from the cliffs into the sea. You are our only hope. By craft, we can overcome Dor Diavo's power. We can substitute you for him and be free again."

BREATHLESSLY she stood before the American. New life seemed to sweep through her as the words poured from her lips. New life and new hope. Color came to her cheeks and fire leaped from her eyes.

"So the wind blows from that direction, eh?" said a heavy voice from the doorway.

King whirled. The door had opened noiselessly. Standing in it, flanked by his guards, stood Dor Diavo.

Sonthia had said the ruler was asleep in his chambers. But Dor Diavo wasn't asleep. He was here.

"I have long suspected there was a plot against me," the ruler continued. "And I was quite sure the plotters would jump at the opportunity to substitute you for me. That's why I had you brought here to this cell and imprisoned, man from Mayan—to lure these would-be rebels out into the open. Otherwise I would have had you killed as soon as you were brought before me."

The ruler laughed.

"I tricked these would be rebels very neatly. And you also, man from Mayan."

King heard a little cry of fear from the girl. The appearance of the ruler and her cry of fear convinced him that she had not been trying to trick him. She was a rebel all right, but she was fighting against a cruel and ruthless ruler.

"Seize them," Dor Diavo grated.

Their guns, and every other piece of metal in their clothes had been removed before they were put in the cell. The guards had obviously not known what the guns were for, but equally obviously they weren't taking any chances. The only weapons Don King and Joe Markham had were their fists. Fists against shields and short swords and lances. Fists against men in armor. Fists against battle-axes.

"Grab that stone bench, Joe," King shouted. "We'll use it as a battering ram and drive straight through them. Sonthia! Get between us. We're not licked yet…"

As he leaped back toward the wall to help Markham lift the heavy stone bench, he looked over his shoulder to make certain the girl had understood what he was going to try to do.

He stopped in mid-stride, his eyes, racing over the small room.

Sonthia was gone.

Seconds earlier she had been there in the room. He had heard her gasp in fear.

But now she was gone. Gone!

Two guards were pressing forward through the only door, swords ready, shields extended. They completely blocked the exit. She could not have slipped between them.

But she was no longer in the room. In the snap of a finger, she had miraculously vanished.

"Golly, Boss," Markham dumfoundedly gasped. "What happened to the girl?"

CHAPTER FIVE
Into Invisibility

STARING at the empty room, Don King stood without moving. He had the bewildering impression that this was only another nightmare from which he would presently awaken. People didn't just vanish, in the snap of a finger, into nothingness. Girls didn't just disappear.

The wild thought was in his mind—perhaps none of this was real. These people had come out of ancient Atlantis, across a maddening gulf of time. Perhaps they existed here in 1940 as illusions, as shadows that had only the seeming of reality, as specters that moved ghost-like through a world in which they had no real existence. Perhaps Sonthia and Dor Diavo and this island kingdom had come out of his own mind. Perhaps he was really a descendant of some long dead Atlantan and he was reliving the experiences of his forebear.

"Sonthia!" he called sharply.

Then was no answer.

"Sonthia!" This time his voice was almost a scream.

No answer came.

She was gone. Like a puff of smoke before the wind, she had vanished into nothingness. Except for Don King and Joe Markham, and the guards pressing through the doorway, the prison cell was empty. Dor Diavo had stepped back into the corridor out of sight and had left his guards to do the dirty work.

"Spit them on your swords!" King heard the ruler order.

There was no time left to wonder what had happened to the girl, to wonder whether this was illusion or reality. The guards were real. King was willing to bet his life on that. It shocked him to realize he *was* betting his life on it.

"Up with the bench, Joe," he yelled.

The sailor was already tugging at the heavy stone seat. As King leaped to help him, he turned up a panic-stricken face.

"It won't come loose, Boss," he whispered. "It's set solid in the floor. It won't come out."

Markham's massive muscles stood out like ropes as he tried to lift the bench. Tried, and failed.

"Look out, Boss," he yelled, looking over King's shoulder.

King whirled. Two of the guards were already in the room. Others were coming through the door.

A sword, held in a brawny arm, was already raised. There was a gloating look on the sadistic face of the man who wielded it.

One stroke with that sharp-edged weapon and King would be cut in two. He would never really know what hit him. He would fall like a sodden lump of flesh, and the angel of death would swoop down for him before he touched the floor.

Glittering, the sword started down toward him. His only chance was to leap in under the blow, drive his fist into the face of the man with the weapon. It was a forlorn hope. He would run directly into the shield. And in the exact center of the shield was a needlepointed metal spike six inches long, placed there for such an emergency as this. Anyone attempting to leap in under the descending sword would be automatically spitted on the spiked shield.

King started to leap. As he moved there was a sudden thump. A red bruise miraculously appeared on the face of the guard. The man staggered. Something in the air seemed to grasp the sword, jerk it out of the guard's hands. It leaped, hilt foremost, straight at King.

The startled guard gazed dumfoundedly at his empty hands. His eyes were wide with sudden fright. One hand automatically went up to the bruise on his cheek. He fingered it uncertainly.

"Here!" a voice hissed at King. "Take the sword. With it we may be able to fight our way out of here."

The voice was speaking from the empty air.

It was Sonthia's voice.

HE couldn't see her. There was a wavering blur in the air but it was so indistinct that he couldn't focus his eyes on it. Looking like the distortion produced by air currents rising above a hot stove, it flowed in and out of his vision so fast he could not be certain he really saw anything, except the sword. There was no doubt that he saw that. The hilt kept jabbing at his hands.

The second guard, perplexed, stared at the sword.

"Take it, Don King," came Sonthia's urgent whisper from nothingness.

"Quickly. It is our only chance."

Don King took the sword. Instantly a bruised place appeared on the face of the second guard. His sword was knocked from his hands. It fell to the floor. It then suddenly seemed to leap upward to Joe Markham.

"This one is for you, Sailor," the voice said. "Now I will get one for myself."

The indistinct blur leaped toward the other guards. There was a clatter and the men seemed to struggle for a minute among themselves. Then a sword detached itself from them, and apparently supported by nothing but air, menaced them from the front.

"At them, Don King!" said Sonthia's voice. "At them, Sailor. Never say die until we're dead."

King still did not realize what had happened. A hoarse shout from one of the guards brought him to his senses.

"The girl!" the guard shouted. "She has a cloak of the Invisible Ones."

There was terror in that shout, far more terror than could be accounted for by the fact that Sonthia, incredible as it was, had become invisible.

"The Invisible Ones!" a white faced guard echoed.

The words threw the men into consternation. A sudden chill seemed to strike them. Their sword points dropped.

King saw the change come over them, but he had no time to wonder about it. The important thing was that at last he understood what had happened to Sonthia. She hadn't vanished into nothingness. She hadn't been snatched back into the old time out of which she and her race had come. She had become invisible, which meant, among other things, that there was hidden somewhere in this Atlantan civilization a marvelous scientific knowledge. The scientists of 1940 did not know how to create invisibility. They were working on it and they would solve it eventually. But they hadn't solved it yet.

More important still, it meant that Sonthia was real. She was no illusion of his own mind, no phantom, no specter. She was real. And this land of Atlantis was real.

Silence fell. The guards looked uneasily and questioningly at each other.

In the corridor outside, Dor Diavo, staying safely out of danger himself, shouted.

"There are no Invisible Ones. Capture them, you mangy dogs. I'll have the head of the first man who refuses to obey orders."

The guards hesitated. They looked nervously at the sword waving in the air in front of them. They were afraid of that sword, they were afraid of the invisible girl who wielded it, they were afraid of the idea of invisibility. But they were more afraid of Dor Diavo.

King got the idea that the Invisible Ones were mythical creatures that the guards, for some reason, feared. Apparently there was a legend among the Atlantans of strange invisible creatures. When an invisible girl had jerked their swords from their hands, they had remembered the legend. They hadn't believed the legend until they saw the sword in the air, just as a man of the Twentieth Century, hearing stories about ghosts, doesn't believe in ghosts—until he sees one. Then he remembers the stories he has heard.

WHETHER or not the guards believed in their Invisible Ones, they had no choice but to believe in Dor Diavo. They knew him. They knew what he would do to them if they disobeyed his orders.

"I said to attack them," the ruler grated. "Spit them on your swords. A reward to the first man who draws blood. Death to the first man who tries to flee. At them, you curs, or I'll have your heads."

"*That* put the old convincer on them," Joe Markham grated. "Here they come, Boss. I never handled one of these pig-stickers before, but here, I guess, is where—I—learn. Ugh!" The sailor grunted. He took one step forward, the sword clasped in both hands. He lifted it over his head and brought it down with all his tremendous strength.

A frantic guard tried to parry the blow. The descending blade knocked his weapon out of his hand. He tried to lift his shield. He never got it up.

The sailor's descending sword bit through the guard's metal helmet. It sliced his head neatly in two.

"Who's next?" Markham grunted, jerking the weapon free. He scorned to pick up the shield of the fallen man. It would only be in his way. He would have to use one hand on the shield and the other on the sword—to hell with that. Joe Markham wanted to use both hands on his pig-sticker.

Don King was already in action. There were eight of the guards. Sonthia had taken the weapons from three of them. Markham had just put one out of this and every other battle to come. That left four. The odds were two to one against them, not counting Sonthia. And God alone knew how many more guards there were with Dor Diavo in the corridor outside.

King parried a sword thrust that would have slit his throat from ear to ear. The guard was using the point, thrusting straight out from the protection of his shield. King ducked and swerved to one side, letting the sword go on over his shoulder. He struck fiercely upward. The arm of the guard was protected by closely linked chain mail, which was all that saved his sword-arm. King's sword bit through the mail and into the muscles. Blood gushed. The guard dropped his sword. He wasn't badly wounded but he was out of the fight.

Three left to go! The odds were lessening.

"Give 'em hell, Boss!" Markham was roaring.

King swung his sword at the nearest guard. The fellow's shield came up and the blade glanced harmlessly from it. He lifted his own weapon for the fierce downward stroke. Another sword flashed through the air, knocking the blade from his hands.

It was Sonthia, fighting beside them, who had struck the sword from the hands of the guard. Sonthia, invisible.

"Good girl!" King called.

Two left to go. The odds were in their favor for the first time.

The odds shifted again, this time entirely in their favor. The guards had not liked this fight. The invisible girl who wielded a sword had almost driven them into a panic. Only the fear of Dor Diavo had kept them from running. Panic caught the two who had been disarmed. Without weapons, they could not hope to fight. They turned and ran. The two who still had their weapons fled with them.

"Come back and fight," Joe Markham yelled, as the guards all tried to get through the door at the same time.

MARKHAM and King they would have been willing to fight. But there was something about the idea of fighting an invisible girl that turned them into cowards.

"We've whipped them!" Sonthia's voice panted from the air.

Dor Diavo's shout sounded from the corridor outside.

"Get back in there and fight!" he screamed.

His men did not obey him. They scrambled through the door.

"Reserves!" the ruler shouted. "Forward."

The tramp of marching feet sounded in the corridor. More guards, coming at the double quick.

"Boss," said Markham nervously. "We better get the hell out of here while we have a chance."

King was thinking the same thing. They might overcome a few of Dor Diavo's men but in the end force of numbers would overcome them. And reinforcements were approaching at the double quick. He grabbed a discarded shield from the floor, fiercely gripped his sword, and started for the door.

"Wait!" Sonthia whispered.

"Come on," King answered. "If we don't make a break for it now, we'll never get another chance. We whipped and scared those guards off once, but we can't do it twice."

"But we will meet them outside," the girl's voice protested. "We have only one chance," she went quickly on. "Throw down your swords and shields."

The sword that she carried, which had been hanging in the air as she held it, fell with a clatter in the corner of the room as she tossed it down.

"But we'll be helpless," King kicked.

"No we won't," Sonthia answered. "I'm going to try to extend the cloak of the Invisible Ones to cover you two. I'm not certain it will work but I am going to try. Quickly!" Her voice was growing desperate with urgency as the pounding of racing feet grew louder outside. "It is difficult to make metal invisible. That is why you must discard your weapons. Hurry...they'll be here in a second. We must be out of the room before they block the door."

She was going to try to make the three of them invisible! If the guards could not see them, they would have a chance to slip through the corridor without being seen. King saw the thin blur of light that was all he could see of Sonthia move toward him, felt her hand nestle into his. He flung the sword and the shield aside. Markham did the same.

King didn't know what Sonthia did. He expected a cloak of some kind to be thrown over him. But the girl did not do that. Her hand gripped his and he heard a thin, far-off vibration. The next second he was gasping for breath.

He was completely lost in blackness. If he had suddenly stepped into a completely dark room, the sensation would have been the same. He couldn't see.

"You will think you have gone blind," Sonthia's whisper reassured him. "Later, I will explain how I can see while you cannot. Now, hold tightly to my hand. I will lead you and the sailor out. Walk on tiptoes. Do not make any noise. Do not talk."

KING felt her pulling him. He followed blindly. His shoulder brushed against the door as they left the room.

"The guards are here," Sonthia's faint whisper came. "We must slip along the wall."

King didn't need to be told that the guards had arrived. He could hear their hoarse voices, the jangle of their equipment. Mostly he could hear the voice of Dor Diavo ordering them to enter the cell. King held his breath, and slid along the wall.

At any second a guard might touch them. An unwary sound might betray them. Sweat ran down King's face. He could not wipe it away. Blindly he slipped along the wall. He heard Markham's husky breathing and whispered fiercely at the sailor to be quiet.

He did not know how far away they were from the cell where they had been held prisoner. Suddenly silence fell behind them. A guard shouted.

"They're not in here."

Instantly Dor Diavo shouted. "The girl has made them invisible. Lock hands and search the cell. Then search the corridor. *Feel* for them. Even if they are invisible, you can feel them. Get moving," the ruler ranted. "If you let them escape, I'll have you beaten to death."

"We'll have to run for it," Sonthia whispered.

CHAPTER SIX
An Irresistible Command

"THIS," Sonthia whispered, "is why I could see while you could not."

She showed them a small device that looked like a pair of dark glasses. "With these, the wearer of the cloak of the Invisible Ones, can see. Unfortunately, I had only a pair for myself."

At least temporarily they had escaped from Dor Diavo and his men. By the time the guards had finished searching the cell and had started feeling their way along the corridor, they were safely out. Sonthia had led them, by devious trails, across the width of the city. She had brought them to a plain, unornamented building standing by itself.

"Show me that cloak of invisibility," said King.

Sonthia was no longer invisible and he was looking keenly at her, trying to see the miraculous garment he knew she possessed. She was clothed in an abbreviated dress. A belt, caught in front with a buckle, circled her slim waist. A single small ornament glittered in the dark coils of her hair. Nowhere could King see anything that resembled a cloak.

"It is only called a cloak," she answered. "It really isn't." She pointed to the buckle on her belt and to the ornament in her hair. "These," she said, "are the cloak of invisibility."

King's doubt showed on his face. Markham, pressing nearer, grunted.

"You do not believe me," she challenged. "Well, see for yourself."

Her hand touched the buckle, pressed lightly against a design worked into the surface. A note, like the sound produced by a tiny harp, throbbed through the air. If King had not been listening closely he wouldn't have heard it.

Before his eyes Sonthia seemed to blur. She smiled at him. Then, in the snap of a finger, she was gone.

"She wasn't fooling us," said Markham, "but how on earth does that belt buckle make her invisible?"

"We'll have to ask her," King answered.

When the girl reappeared, they questioned her.

"I don't know how it works," she answered. "The invisible cloak is made in many ways. Almost always it resembles an ornament that anyone might wear without attracting attention. It might be a finger ring, or a necklace, or a bracelet. In my case, it is two ornaments. One will not work without the other. So far as I know, I have the only invisible cloak in existence now. Once there were many of them, but all have been lost except mine. I didn't let anyone know that I possessed the cloak. They were made, in the long ago, by the Invisible Ones."

As she spoke the words a shadow of fear crossed her face.

"Who are the Invisible Ones?" King asked.

The fear on her face grew deeper.

"No one knows anymore," she whispered. "They existed long ago. The legends say they were the gods of our race and that in the long ago they lived with our people and went daily among men. Then our people forgot their gods and became evil and in return the gods hid themselves from the sight of men." She hesitated. "I do not know whether this is true or not. It happened many thousands of years before I was born. I think it is probable that the Invisible Ones were extremely wise men and that they learned, among other things, the secret of invisibility. I think probably our rulers in that long gone time grew jealous of the power of the wise men, and tried to conquer them, and the wise men hid themselves. Our legends say that the Invisible Ones still exist, that they come and go among us, hidden from our sight, punishing the wicked and rewarding the good. But I do not know. No one knows. No one of my generation has ever seen an Invisible One."

"They must have existed once," said King. "Your possession of that cloak proves it."

"I had the cloak from my mother, who had it from her mother. It's very old."

KING nodded. It was the age-old fight between science and politics, each seeking to rule the world. He did not doubt that the Invisible Ones had been the scientists of the ancient Atlantans. The scientists had gained too much power and the rulers had fought them and the scientists had hidden themselves away.

"This," said Sonthia, "is the temple of the Invisible Ones. You will be safe here. Even Dor Diavo will not trespass on these sacred premises. I, myself, scarcely dared to come here. But there was no other place to go, and I could not permit Dar Diavo to recapture you."

The shadow of fear was again on her face. King guessed how much courage it had taken to bring them here. She, too, had a superstitious awe of the gods—or mighty men—of her race. She did not like to trespass in their sacred places.

"Brave girl," said King.

"Do you think we're safe here?" Markham asked uneasily. "Somehow I don't like this place, Boss. It's full of—ghosts."

The sailor had been examining the temple of the Invisible Ones. It was a small building constructed of marble, entirely unornamented. It was full of shadows that seemed to flow with a strange liquid life of their own.

"This is the only place where we are safe," Sonthia answered. "As soon as the search dies down, we will find a boat and escape."

"But what about the rebellion?" King asked.

"It is lost," the girl answered. "Now that Dor Diavo knows there is a plot against him, he will be constantly on the alert. If we remain here, he will certainly find us in time. It will not be pleasant to be in the power of our ruler," she finished, her voice trembling.

King nodded. He did not need to guess what their fate would be if Dor Diavo captured them.

"What about your friends? You indicated others were with you in the plot to rebel. Won't Dor Diavo make things hot for them?"

"He doesn't know who they are. They will be safe enough, but our only hope is to escape. Can we not return to your land, Don King? Even Dor Diavo will not dare to follow us there."

"We not only can, we will," King answered. "And then we'll return here."

"Return here! Come back to the land where Dor Diavo rules?"

"Yes. With a hundred fighting men behind us, armed with rifles and submachine guns. Joe, do you know any husky lads who might be willing to do a little fighting?"

"I can get two hundred, if you want that many," Markham answered. "All I'll have to do is go down to the docks, Boss," the sailor grinned, "we'll show Dor Diavo a thing or two about fighting."

"I'll say we will," King answered grimly. "But right now our only hope is to get out of here. Sonthia, lead the way to those boats. And be ready to make us invisible if we run into anybody."

King's pulse was leaping. At last they were in the clear. If they could escape—and with the aid of Sonthia's cloak of invisibility, there was little chance that they would fail—and return with a boat crammed to the rails with fighting men, then they could rescue this pitiful remnant of a vanished people from the dictator who ruled them.

And the Atlantans had much that they could give the world. Their history, stretching back into the mists of time, would be invaluable to science. Their knowledge, that clever device which generated invisibility, would be eagerly added to Twentieth Century science.

Don King could lead his lost people to their rightful heritage. He could not fail. Against high-powered rifles the armor and weapons of the guards of Dor Diavo would be worthless.

CAUTIOUSLY, every sense alert, they started out of the temple. Here and there in the city they would hear the guards searching for them.

"They'll have a sweet time finding us when we're invisible," Markham muttered.

Then a voice, speaking somewhere from the shadows around them, said harshly.

"Don King!"

The American jumped. His eyes darted from shadow to shadow, seeking the person who had spoken. He saw no one. His two companions looked at him.

"Who is it?" Sonthia said. "Did you see someone?"

"What's the matter, Boss?" Markham asked. "What did you jump like that for?"

"Someone called my name," King answered. He was aware that a sticky wash of perspiration had suddenly appeared in the palms of his hands.

"I heard no one," Sonthia said.

"Nobody said anything," Markham added. "You must have been hearing things, Boss."

"I know what I heard," King answered.

"Don King," the voice said again.

King whirled. The voice had seemed to come from behind him this time. He saw nothing. But the perspiration that had made his hands sticky was now spreading over his whole body.

"There it was again," he said.

"But no one spoke," Sonthia insisted, a note of desperate fear suddenly creeping into her voice.

"I didn't hear anything," Markham said uneasily.

"Seize the girl, Don King," the voice grated. *"Choke the treacherous she-devil to death."*

Then King realized what was happening. He was the reincarnation of Dor Diavo. And Dor Diavo, being the older incarnation, had power over him. Even when Dor Diavo had not known that he existed, the ruler's vagrant thought impulses, transmitted across thousands of miles of space, had been powerful enough to instill in King a wanderlust so strong he could not resist it. The *rapport* between the two men had been erratic, not subject to control, but when the ruler had raged at those who had opposed him, King's arms and legs had obeyed Dor Diavo's orders.

Now Dor Diavo had realized the power he held over the American. He was using it to order King to choke Sonthia to death. It was Dor Diavo's voice that King heard. The ruler was not present. He was somewhere else in the city, and his thought impulses were being transmitted to King's mind.

Sweat was pouring down King's face.

Sonthia's startled cry showed that she realized what was happening. The girl cowered away from him. Markham stood, indecision on his scarred face, staring in hopeless perplexity at the man whom he called master.

"Boss," the sailor whispered. "What's the matter with you? Why do you look at Sonthia like that, Boss?"

KING felt that old, incredible, helpless feeling creep over him. His muscles began to jerk, to lump into knots. His will power seemed to be leaving him. And he was helpless to prevent it.

"Fight, Don King," Sonthia whispered. "Fight!"

"I'm fighting," King gritted from between clenched teeth. Only he knew how violently he was fighting. Because the struggle was purely mental, involving no physical action, it was no less terrible. King stood in a half crouch, feet planted wide apart, arms drawn up for defense, fighting the control that was trying to clamp itself on to his mind, fighting Dor Diavo, fighting his other self.

"Damn you, Dor Diavo!" he ground out.

Somewhere in his mind the ruler laughed.

"Fight, Don King," he jeered. "Try and fight! The older incarnation has power over the younger. You are the younger, Don King. Fight like the very devil was after you. Fight!"

Sweat poured in a flood over King's body.

"Seize the girl, Don King," Dor Diavo's voice came whispering in his mind. Seize her!"

King took one step toward Sonthia. She shrank before him.

"Please, Don," she begged, her eyes wide with fright.

"I'm trying, Sonthia," he gasped.

He took a second step toward her. His legs were moving against his will. His hands were coming up, fingers spread like claws.

He was two men. The real Don King would not under any circumstances have harmed Sonthia. The minute he first saw her the real Don King had known that, if he had sought the vanished colonies of his people in Egypt and Central America, he had also sought something else— Sonthia. He had been seeking this girl out of ancient Atlantis. He had found her.

And Dor Diavo was forcing him to kill her.

"Fight!" the ruler jeered.

"Damn you—" King groaned.

He took the third step toward the girl. His fingers closed around her throat.

"Choke the she-devil," the sneering ruler ordered, his voice whispering in King's brain.

"Please, Don," she whispered, her face white in the shadows. "Don, I love you. Look at me, Don. Please, for my sake, fight!"

King groaned. His hands were no longer under his control. He realized what he was doing but he could not control his body. His fingers began to close around her throat.

He was going to choke her to death, he was going to kill her with his bare hands. And there was nothing he could do about it.

Shadows seemed to march across his mind. The shadows in the temple of the Invisible Ones seemed to swirl in circles.

Dor Diavo's laugh sounded.

"You're doing a good job, Don King," he gloated. "I couldn't throttle her better myself. See how her hands are tearing at your fingers, trying to pull them from her throat. See how her face is turning purple, her eyes bulging. Hear how she chokes. Note how her struggles are growing weaker. She won't last much longer, Don King.

"After she is dead, do you know what I am going to do to you? No, I'm not going to kill you. That would be too easy—for you. I'm going to imprison you, so you can remember all the rest of your life how you choked to death the girl who would have been your sweetheart. Isn't it clever of me, Don King, to think of that. *Heh, heh, heh...*" The ruler's laugh whispered evilly in King's brain.

KING turned a tortured face toward Joe Markham. The sailor was frightened almost out of his wits. His lips were moving in prayer and his face was seamed with terror. He did not understand what was happening.

To him it seemed that King had suddenly gone crazy.

"*Slug me!*" King whispered.

"W-what?" the sailor stammered.

"Hit me!" King rasped. "I'm not choking Sonthia because I want to. Hit me! Knock me out! It's the only way to save her life."

The girl's struggles had grown weaker.

"You mean that?" Markham gasped.

"I never meant anything more in my life," King answered. "You're not a reincarnation of Dor Diavo. He doesn't have control over you. Knock me out before he sends guards here."

Markham swung a ham-like fist. It drove straight to the point of King's jaw, sent a flash of white-hot pain through his brain. His fingers loosened. He staggered backward, collided with a column, fell to the floor. He wasn't out. He was dazed. And as he staggered and fell, he was laughing—with happiness. He had thwarted Dor Diavo. He had saved Sonthia's life.

"Save the girl," he whispered to Joe Markham. "Take care of her. Never mind me. And if I try to attack you again, knock the hell out of me."

The sailor was already bending over Sonthia. She had fallen when King released her.

Whispering in King's mind from the distance came Dor Diavo's roar of rage.

"Damn you, King, you tricked me," the ruler snarled. "I deliberately left part of your mind free so you would know what you were doing. I wanted you to know you were killing her. But you tricked me. Well, trick me now, damn you!"

King felt a merciless pressure close over his mind. He tried to fight against it, but it clamped down like a vise. His brain felt like it was being squeezed as Dor Diavo tightened his control to exclude Don King's mind from his body.

"Get to your feet," the ruler snarled. "Destroy that treacherous she-devil. If that sailor tries to stop you, whip him. Beat him with your fists. But kill the girl. Do you understand me? Kill her!"

Slowly King came erect. His face was now utterly blank. All trace of the personality of the real Don King was gone from it. It was frozen, lifeless, like the face of a robot, or a zombie. And when he moved it was with the staggering, lifeless lurch of the zombie, of the living dead.

Markham glanced up as he approached.

"Get away from me, Boss," the sailor said.

King did not answer.

"Boss, I said for you to stay away," the sailor warned.

King kept coming. Lurching zombie-like, he advanced toward the pair.

"Kill them," Dor Diavo's voice shrieked in his brain.

MARKHAM rose to his feet. He lifted his fist.

King then struck with all the speed of a striking cobra. His left hand lanced out like a small battering ram. It struck the surprised sailor at the base of the ear and on the corner of the jaw. All of King's weight was behind this blow.

Markham had not been expecting the blow. His effort to hit King had only been half-hearted at best. He didn't want to hit his boss. Don King struck with all the pent up fury of Dor Diavo. King's mind seethed with the ruler's overpowering lust to kill. Don King was no longer Don King. He was Dor Diavo. And he struck as Dor Diavo would have struck if he had had the opportunity and the ability.

Markham went down like a stunned ox.

King turned toward the girl.

"You're next," Dor Diavo's voice rasped from his lips. "You rebelled against me—and I'm sure you must know the penalty for that. You wanted Don King to cuddle you in his arms, didn't you?" A twinkle came to Diavo's eyes.

"Well, get ready. He's going to cuddle you in a way you will never forget." The ruler laughed. King moved toward the helpless girl.

She was conscious now. Her face was still purple from the choking she had received but she was recovering rapidly.

"Please, Don..." she whispered.

King's fingers reached for her.

And closed on empty air. Her hand darted toward the ornament at her waist, the tiny flute-note sounded, a fluorescent blur folded over her. She had become invisible.

King stopped. He couldn't see her.

"Feel for her!" the ruler's raging voice rasped in his brain.

King obeyed. He couldn't find her.

"I wish you to throttle the unconscious sailor," the ruler blurted out in a sinister tone. "Then come to me. My guards will find the girl all right. Throttle the sailor and come to me."

King then turned toward Joe Markham. He was just in time to see the sailor's body suddenly blur into invisibility as Sonthia extended the cloak of the Invisible Ones over him.

"All right," Dor Diavo rasped. "My guards will find them. You come to me, Don King. I have something waiting for you."

On leaden feet Don King turned slowly and walked from the temple of the long-gone Invisible Ones. His mind at this point was a complete blank. He wasn't cognizant of what he was doing. All he knew was that he was obeying an order that he could not resist. He had no inkling of what waited for him at the hands of Dor Diavo.

As he walked out of the temple the shadows seemed to blur around him, shadows as dark as the shadows in his mind.

CHAPTER SEVEN
The Invisible Ones

"WHICH form of death do you prefer, man from Mayan?" Dor Diavo questioned. "Would you like the death that comes from having a needle thrust slowly past and through the eyeball, would you prefer the death from serpents, would you like to be beaten to death, and would you perhaps choose the death that comes from having molten lead poured slowly down your throat?"

They were in a room in the place to which King, moving like a walking dead man, had come. There Dor Diavo, flanked by guards, had waited for him. Guards were constantly coming and going as they reported the progress of the search for Sonthia and Markham. The uncanny hypnosis that had settled down over King's mind had been relaxed. His brain was clear, so that he clearly understood what was happening. But he had no control over his body.

Dor Diavo preferred it that way. He had deliberately relaxed his uncanny control over the man who was his reincarnation so King could understand what was happening.

King's face was expressionless. He stood without moving. Only his eyes were alive. And they seemed to be filled with tiny flakes of flame.

King saw the sadism on Dor Diavo's face. The ruler would derive great pleasure from torturing him. And in Dor Diavo's easy enumeration of different horrible ways of inflicting death, King saw that torture was no new thing in this world. He saw why Sonthia had rebelled against this ruler, why the Atlantans themselves must have always been on the verge of rebellion. And, if Dor Diavo was a fair sample of the rulers of the old time, he saw why the ancient scientists had hidden themselves away in invisibility. Even in a civilized world, the death of a criminal was sometimes necessary. But civilization tried to make that death as easy as possible.

Dor Diavo was just the opposite. He preferred to make death as hideous as possible, as cruel as the mind could devise.

In every human being there is both good and evil. King was the personification of what is best in the human race, Dor Diavo of what is worst.

"Make up your mind," the ruler rasped. "Which way do you prefer to die?"

"Does it make any difference, which I prefer?" King answered. There was defiance in his voice.

The ruler was taken aback. It had been his experience that men crawled before him, begged in whining voices for the boon of an easy death. But here was a man who did not crawl.

"You dare to defy me?" he shouted.

"No," King answered levelly. "I do not defy you. You are *beneath* defiance."

Dor Diavo's face flamed scarlet with anger.

"I will show you whether you can trick me into giving you an easy death," he said.

"I am not trying to trick you into anything," King answered. "Do with me as you will. There is nothing I can do to oppose you."

HE MEANT it. He was no longer concerned about himself. Even if he had a chance, he could not escape, for Dor Diavo, exerting his terrible mental power, could call him back. Nor would King fight. Dor Diavo held him powerless. His only remaining hope was that Sonthia and Markham had had time to escape. If Sonthia could reach the boat as she promised, Markham could sail it. And they should have had time to reach the boat by now. They had certainly not been captured or the guards would have brought them here.

"Very well, Don King," Dor Diavo snapped. I have decided what to do with you."

"And what is that?"

"You will commit suicide," Dor Diavo answered, "by drinking molten lead."

"I will not!" King started to say. Then he realized that if Dor Diavo willed him to drink molten lead, he would drink it. There was nothing he could do to prevent it. His mind was now his own and he could talk. But he could not move another muscle of his body. He could not even lift his hand to wipe the sweat from his face.

But—to die from drinking molten lead!

There was a horrible choking sensation in his throat. He coughed, and choked.

At the wave of Dor Diavo's hand two guards went racing off. They returned quickly, bearing with them a small cauldron in which a grayish mass of metal was smoking. The lead had been taken from a fire. Apparently it was always kept ready.

Swiftly the guards set up a tripod, hung the cauldron on it, built a fire. The blaze licked up around the edges of the pot.

King stared with horrible fascination at the metal. The pot was small. It did not hold over a pint. It would come back to a boil all the quicker because of the small quantity. There would not be enough for more than a single draught.

One draught would be enough.

"It comes to a boil," Dor Diavo said. "Look at it, man who would take my place. See the bubbles already forming on the surface. It will warm your stomach!" the ruler laughed. "It will warm your gullet as it goes down."

The guards laughed with him. They were looking forward with evident enjoyment to what was coming.

Sweat ran down King's forehead and got in his eyes, making them smart with salty pain. Desperately he tried to move himself but not even his little finger would answer to his will. He could only stare at that horribly bubbling cauldron. He saw the guards bring in a small cup with a long handle. The lead would be poured into that and the cup handed to him.

The lead was boiling freely now.

"Pour the draught," Dor Diavo ordered.

THE cauldron was tipped and the molten metal ran in a gray stream into the cup. Holding it with tongs, the guards brought the cup to King.

"Take it," Dar Diavo rasped. "Drink deep, Don King, because it will be a long time before you have another chance to quench your thirst."

Involuntarily, against his will, King's right hand went out toward the handle of the cup.

This was the end. There was nothing he could do to help himself. His hand moved against his will. And against his will, his hand would carry the cup to his lips, his mouth would gulp at the molten metal, a searing blaze would race down his throat. *Then,* in all probability Dor Diavo would release his body, at least partly, so he and his guards could enjoy the death agonies of this helpless man.

King reached for the cup.

"You must release this man, Dor Diavo," a voice said. "You must sever the chain that binds him to you, you must dissolve the mental bond by which you control him."

The voice spoke from the air.

It was not Sonthia's voice, nor was it the voice of Joe Markham. It was no voice that King had ever heard before.

It froze into instant silence every sound in the room. Dor Diavo's' face went blotchy white. His eyes darted over his guards.

"Who spoke?" he demanded.

The guards shifted uneasily.

"Which one of you said that?" the ruler rasped.

"None of my men spoke, your majesty," their captain answered.

"Don't lie to me. I heard someone speak. Who was it?"

"We spoke," the voice said.

In front of King's eyes, directly between him and the ruler, the air seemed to blur. Far-off, a tiny harp note throbbed. The blur dissolved. Three people stood there, two men and a woman.

They were clad all in white. At a glance it was obvious that they were old, incredibly old. Later, King would wonder what made him think these three people were old. It was not their skin. That was smooth and flawless, a delicate brown color. Nor were their faces wrinkled. It was their eyes, he decided, and the calmness with which they stood before Dor Diavo. Their eyes were old. All passions and all hates had been washed out of their eyes, and all fear. Only compassion remained, and a wisdom that was beyond the understanding, a wisdom so deep and so ancient that it was appalling.

Who were they, King wondered. Where had they come from? Why had they appeared here?

"The Invisible Ones!" a guard gasped.

The Invisible Ones! The gods of Atlantan legend, or the scientists of ancient Atlantis, who had lost a battle in the old time and had hidden themselves away. They hadn't perished. They hadn't died. Or at least all of them hadn't. They had come forward into the new time, come across the maddening gulf of time with Dor Diavo when he had fled the tragedy that had destroyed their homeland. They had come into this new world, still invisible, still hidden away.

And now they were revealing themselves...

"We spoke," they seemed to say all together. "It has been our policy never to interfere with the rulers of Atlantis, for we have learned that in most instances the people of a land receive exactly the government they deserve. If the rulers are bad, it is because the people are bad. Nor can an outside force, such as we represent, lift the people up. They must lift themselves. For that reason, we have never before interfered with an Atlantan ruler.

"But now has come one who would lead the remnant of our people upward instead of down. You, Dor Diavo, would destroy that one. We shall not interfere to prevent you from doing this, if you can. But you must fight a fair battle. Therefore, Dor Diavo, you must dissolve the mental bond by which you control Don King—"

IN these words, softly spoken, King caught a glimpse of a keen justice working inscrutably to reach its own ends. The Invisibles would set him free—to fight. They would not fight his battles for him. That was wisdom. That was justice. A man must stand on his own feet and fight. That was what King wanted.

The face of the ruler was blotchy. He stared incredulously at the three calm figures facing him. He seemed to think he was being tricked. He looked like a sullen boy suddenly in fear of punishment, but doubting if he can be punished.

"Do you accept?" the three questioned.

"Seize them!" the ruler rasped at his guards.

His men had little stomach for the business. But when their captain barked an order at them, they started forward.

One of the three invisibles turned toward the guards. There was nothing hurried in his movements. He glanced at the men coming toward him. Something flashed in his hand as he waved it.

The guards stopped. A wave of force seemed to flow out to them. They stopped.

The Invisible One turned back to the ruler.

"So we must force you, Dor Diavo?" they said, still speaking in that strange unison that sounded like a single voice. "Well, so be it."

One of them took from under his robe a little crystal box. He opened the lid. A tiny arrangement of crystals, sparkling like glass beads strung on silver wire, unfolded from the interior of the box.

"Your control of Don King is based on telepathic hypnosis," the three said. "And telepathy is transmitted as is" (here they glanced at King) "radio in the land from which you came. Telepathy is in fact a form of mental radio.* Your mind and the mind of Dor Diavo are tuned to each other, his is the transmitter, yours the receiver. We will merely distort the tuning, so that you will no longer receive the radiations transmitted from his mind."

A tinkling, silver note came from the crystal antennae. It chimed, and chimed again, making a note like the harmony that would come from the tuning fork of an elf.

"That is all," the three said.

The throbbing harp sounded:

A blur of light seemed to fold around the three.

They faded into nothingness.

DOR DIAVO stood like a man in a trance, his blotched face working and distorted, his eyes blinking as if to dispel an illusion from his mind. He seemed to fight to gain control of himself.

"An illusion!" he snarled. "A trick of some kind. There was nothing here. King, I command you. Drink that cup of molten lead."

King had taken the dipper in his hands. The long handle was hot. It seared his fingers but he held on to it.

----

* It has long been suggested that mental waves are emanated by the brain, and that it would be possible to pick up these waves by mechanical means, such as ultra-short radio. Obviously, in Atlantis, the scientists of 14,000 years ago, carried forward by the Invisible Ones, had devised a method of doing this. Thus, they were able to tune in on the mental vibrations of Don King, and of Dor Diavo, and so influence them with interference that a change in wavelength resulted. After this, Dor Diavo was unable to get his own mind in rapport with Don King's, and his control was gone.—Ray Palmer, Ed.

"Yes, Your Majesty," he answered. There was awry, wretched smile on his face. His throat worked as if the lead were already burning it. He lifted the cup.

His hand came back in a sinuous motion. He flung the dipper of molten metal straight at Dor Diavo!

"Try some of your own medicine, you dirty devil!"

The instant the tinkling, silver note had come from the crystal antennae on the little box, King had felt the hypnosis relax. For an instant a keen agony fluttered through his brain, like hundreds of microscopic knives severing nerve connections, breaking synapses, changing subtly the flow of nervous currents through his mind. For a second, while that tiny tuning fork throbbed, the microscopic knives seemed to slice through his brain. Then the note died, and the flashing pain was gone.

The control that chained King's body went with it. Gone, that leaden heaviness in his mind. Gone, that cramped pain in his muscles. Gone, Dor Diavo's control!

He was free. *Free!*

Free to fling at the leering ruler the molten death he had been condemned to drink!

Droplets of lead swirled from the cup. All of the contents didn't touch Dor Diavo. The dipper itself missed. But drops of the molten metal struck him. Unlike his guards, he was not in armor. Metal splashed on his face, his hands, his arms.

His scream rilled through the air like a dagger of sound.

"How do you like your own medicine?" Don King grated.

Dor Diavo slapped at the drops of molten metal. He looked like a man suddenly possessed by demons. He squalled, and throwing himself on the floor, rolled over and over as he tried to get away from the fire that was burning him, the fire that he had intended for King.

His men leaped forward to help him. King knew what would happen next. Dor Diavo wasn't badly hurt. His burns were painful but not serious. As soon as he recovered from his shock he would be in a raging fury. King turned to run. His one thought was to hide until he could contact the three Invisible Ones, or, failing in that, until he could find Sonthia and Markham.

"Grab that man!" he heard Dor Diavo yell. "Don't let him escape."

King headed toward the door. Guards leaped to cut him off. They got to the exit before he did. A line of sharp sword points blocked his escape. His body was free of Dor Diavo's control, but he was still trapped. Trapped! He skidded to a stop.

"This time you won't escape," Dor Diavo raged.

The ruler, angry red blotches on his face where the lead had struck him, had regained his feet and was stalking toward the American. There had never been any pity on Dor Diavo's face. Now it was suffused with a blinding rage.

"I guess you win after all," said King.

"I'm damned if that's so," a heavy voice said. "Here, Boss, take this."

There was a commotion among the guards. A bulky body seemed to force its way through their ranks. King could not see the body. But he could see two things moving toward him. They were hanging in the air.

Pistols! His and Markham's pistol. And it had been Markham's voice who spoke.

"Take the gun, Boss," the sailor said, his voice coming from thin air. "We'll make these monkeys wish they had never been born."

King grabbed one of the guns. Simultaneously he saw a sword tear itself out of the hand of a guard, and he knew that Sonthia, having secured the weapons the Atlantans had taken from them, had come to rescue him. They only had two pistols so Sonthia had to use a sword.

Thunderous blasts of pistol fire roared through the room.

CHAPTER EIGHT
In the Grip of the Kra-kor

"LORD, Boss!" Joe Markham gasped. "Those shields are made of better metal than I thought. Bullets don't go through them."

Dor Diavo, the second he had seen the guns appear, had guessed what was happening. He had promptly dived behind his men and then had leaped to the protection of a heavy stone pillar. From the protection of this he ordered his men to charge. His men obeyed. They didn't for a minute like to face the thundering guns, but obedience had been beaten into them. The guards in front of the door held their positions. The others advanced, shields up, swords ready. A circle of grim-faced men closed in around the two. Sonthia had broken contact with Markham and he had become visible. And because the two men were visible, the girl had chosen to become visible also.

King fired at the advancing men. The Atlantan at whom he had been aiming ducked behind his shield. The heavy slug whanged into the metal and ricocheted violently across the room.

"Is something wrong with your weapons?" Sonthia asked nervously.

"Boss, we better get to hell out of here," Markham added.

King turned toward the door.

"Fire at their legs, he said grimly. "If we can knock down the guards at the door, we'll have a chance to escape."

The legs of the Atlantans were protected by mail, but it did not have the thickness of the shields. King sent a bullet screaming into the men at he door. He aimed low.

A guard toppled.

"That's the stuff!" King shouted. "Aim low. Knock their legs out from under them. We'll have a chance to escape yet."

He fired again. The gun in Markham's hand crashed in unison with his. A ragged hole opened in the ranks of the Atlantans.

"Through that hole!" King ordered. "Joe, you go first. Then Sonthia. I'll bring up the rear."

Like a fullback smashing through tackle, the sailor hit the hole. Frantically the guards tried to close it up. Markham's gun exploded twice. Then it clicked on an empty cartridge. Clubbing it, the sailor struck at the men opposing him.

King, looking back over his shoulder, saw the guards, urged on by Dor Diavo, racing across the room toward them. Only seconds remained to fight their way through the men at the door. Seconds!

"Come on, Boss," Markham yelled. "There's a hole here big enough to drive a truck through."

The sailor, fighting like a cornered lion, had cleared the way. King shoved Sonthia through and into the clear. He dived behind her.

"Quickly," the girl said. "We must get away."

They raced through the door and into the night. Behind them shouts sounded as Dor Diavo organized his men for pursuit.

"The boat!" Sonthia panted. "It is this way."

King hesitated.

"What about the Invisible Ones?" he asked. "Can't we go to them? Won't they help us? And incidentally, how did they happen to turn up so pat the first time?"

"Sonthia found them," Markham answered. "They were in their temple. From what they said, they had been there all the time, only nobody ever knew it because they hadn't wanted to be seen. She got our guns for us too. Slipped into the prison and found them."

"But won't they help us against Dor Diavo?" King answered.

"No," the girl answered. "They said that if we deserved to overcome him, we would succeed. If our hearts were pure and our motives worthy, we would win out. They were only willing to release the control Dor Diavo had over you. Everything else we must do for ourselves. I doubt if they would ever reveal themselves to us again."

"The boat is about our only chance, Boss," Markham said. "Sonthia brought the guns but she didn't know to bring the extra cartridges. All the shells we've got are what's left in the guns, and mine is already empty. We better grab that boat and take a flier out of here. Once we get out on the shipping lanes, we're sure to be picked up."

"All right," King assented. "But we'll come back."

"You damned right we will," the sailor answered. "If I understand this thing right, I had a double back here too. Dor Diavo killed him, which leaves me with a little score of my own to settle."

THE guards were again ranging through the city after them. Creeping stealthily along, following back streets and avoiding the main thoroughfare, slipping along the edges of the dark canals, they reached the boat.

King had been expecting to find something like a galley that they would have to row. The best he had hoped for was a light sailing craft. Instead Sonthia led them to a sleek-hulled little vessel that looked like a sea-going launch. King stared at it in perplexity.

"You were expecting a barge?" the girl asked. "A vessel with slaves to row it? Dor Diavo uses such a craft occasionally, but only to impress us with the fact that he is our ruler. His barge that the slaves row is for state occasions, but when anyone is sent to sea, we use these little ships. Dor Diavo invented them just before the catastrophe in the old time. They carry their own power and move very swiftly."

"Do you know how to operate it?" King questioned.

"Certainly. You merely press buttons and it goes. But get in quickly. Dor Diavo's men may find us at any minute."

They entered the boat. Under the girl's skilled fingers, it slid along the dark canals, passed through the tremendous pool where the sailing vessel on which they had taken passage from New York still floated, and started toward the dark exit that led out to the open sea.

Just as they approached the opening, a shrill hail sounded.

"They've seen us!" King snapped. "Open this thing up and get us out of here before they start after us."

He had been holding his breath for fear they would be seen. Now it had happened.

Sonthia gave the little craft all the power it had. Whatever was the source of energy utilized to drive the vessel, it was most efficient. A powerful roar came from the interior. The launch lifted its nose, and sending rolling a great bow wave, raced through the opening and out to the open sea.

"We're away!" Joe Markham gloated. "We've got 'em beat by a mile. They'll never be able to catch us now. We're loose."

There was ringing exultation in the sailor's voice.

The dark island slipped behind them.

"We've got 'em licked, Boss," Markham gloated again.

As if in refutation there came, from the darkness of the island they were leaving, a cry.

"Kra-*kor!*"

Shrill and clear, it came winging across the waters.

"Kra—*kor!*"

"THE monster!" Markham gasped. "The thing that grabbed our ship. I'd forgotten all about it."

"I hadn't," King said grimly. He stood up and looked back. There was nothing he could see. The thing was too far away as yet. But he could hear it splashing behind them. And he could also hear the throb of another powerboat following them.

The pursuit was already organized. The Atlantans were coming. And they were bringing that incredible sea creature that had attacked and destroyed the stout sailing vessel.

"Can we out run it?" King whispered to Sonthia.

She shook her head. "It swims faster than anything in the ocean. No, Don King, we cannot run faster than it can."

"Kra—*kor...* " The cry came again. It was closer now, the splashes louder.

King looked helplessly around them. He had possibly two shots remaining in his gun. And he knew, from previous experience, that no pistol slug would harm that monstrous sea beast.

Sonthia stood up.

"I am sorry, Don King," she said, "that it has to end like this. But Dor Diavo has won. Nothing can help us here, not even the Invisible Ones."

"I'm sorry, too, Sonthia," King said. His mind was racing, seeking a way to escape. Sonthia might make them invisible, but even invisibility would not keep them from drowning. They might turn the launch and attempt to ram the coming monster, but he knew, from the way it had held the sailing ship, that the launch would not damage it. They could not even turn and attempt to reach the shore. They hadn't a chance.

"What is that thing?" he said to Sonthia, as the cry came again.

"It— I do not know how to explain it," she answered. "Dor Diavo invented it."

"What's that?" King demanded. "Dor Diavo invented it. Then it isn't alive?"

"No. It is made out of metal and therefore cannot be alive. It is like—what do you say?—it is like a robot. It is a—thing—not—alive but with the ability to understand and obey orders."

The sea beast was a robot! It wasn't flesh and blood. It was a cleverly constructed imitation of a gigantic octopus, with steel tentacles. No doubt it was powered the same way the launches were.

"Stop the launch!" King said.

His two companions stared at him.

"Y—you mean, kick it wide open, don't you, Boss? Y—you don't mean to stop it! What we want is to go faster," Markham quavered.

"I said to stop it and I meant what I said."

"B—but we'll only die quicker," Sonthia wailed. "Why should we stop the boat? What are you going to do?"

King told them his plan.

"It's our only chance," he said desperately. "It's got to work. If it doesn't we'll die a few minutes quicker, but we're going to die anyhow. Stop the launch."

Sonthia cut the controls. The roar of the engine died into silence. The launch wallowed in the long sea swell.

"Kra—*kor*..."

There was now in its call the same note that sounds in the bugling of the hound hot on the scent of fleeing prey.

"Boss, I hope you know what you're doin'," Markham said.

"So do I," King said. "But if I don't, it's been nice knowing you, Joe. I might mention that I never hope to meet a braver man."

"T—thanks, Boss."

THE black bulk of the robot was now clearly visible in the heaving waters, the elongated flattish body somewhat resembling the hull of a submarine. The great tentacles were sending up tremendous splashes as they beat the surface of the sea.

"Here goes nothing," King thought. He was surprised to find that he was completely calm. He held up his arm. His fingers were steady, his hand as solid as a rock. His one wish was that he had a cigarette.

"Kra—*kor*..." the screaming note came.

The tip of a tentacle came up out of the water, fingering through the air. The monster was upon them.

"Down in the bottom of the boat," King hissed. "Stay out of the way of those tentacles."

He knew only too well the tremendous strength that reposed in those steel cables.

At his order Sonthia and Markham dropped to the bottom of the launch. King threw himself down beside them.

Tremendous splashes sounded as the robot came up to the boat. Tentacles came over the edge of the launch, circled the hull of the stout little vessel, almost lifted it out of the water.

King was holding his breath. Would those tentacles finger them out, tear them to pieces before he had a chance to try his plan? This was the moment of greatest danger.

The tentacles did not come down into the bottom of the launch!

King breathed easier. "Kra—*kor,*" the robot called.

It did not try to move. It merely held the launch and waited for the powerboat that was coming, the boat that contained Dor Diavo and his men.

King rose on one knee.

"Luck, Boss," Joe Markham whispered.

"God go with you," Sonthia added.

King stood up. He was ready to drop back if a tentacle moved. But the steel cables remained quiet. Across the water he heard the throb of the approaching powerboat.

"It has them!" he heard Dor Diavo exclaim. There was jubilance in his voice, and a gloating note that sent shivers of horror down King's spine.

BESIDE THE BOAT he could see the black hulk of the body of the robot floating in the water. Slowly, cautiously, King drew himself up to the rail. With a single motion he leaped overboard, landing directly on top of the robot.

"Fish Catcher," he said. "You have caught the wrong fish. This is not the fish you were told to catch. The one you want is there, coming toward you." He pointed toward the approaching boat.

That was King's plan. This sea monster was a robot. It possessed a rudimentary intelligence, enough to enable it to obey orders. And if King had judged Dor Diavo correctly, that wily ruler had constructed the robot so it would obey him and no one else. It would react to Dor Diavo's voice, to his commands, and to no other. The ruler would have been extremely unlikely to construct the robot so it would obey anyone else, because then it might have been used against him.

But Don King was the reincarnation of Dor Diavo. In voice, appearance, weight, and build, they were so nearly identical that it was almost impossible to tell the difference between them.

Would the robot be able to tell the difference?
Would it obey King as readily as it obeyed Dor Diavo?

THE creature gurgled horribly. It did not move. It did not obey him.

It seemed to protest, and its cry sounded subdued and doubtful.

"Fish catcher!" King snarled. "You have caught the wrong fish. The other fish is the one you want."

"Kra—kor." The thing answered.

King's heart was up in his mouth. Was the creature going to obey him?

Out of the corner of his eyes, he saw the launch carrying Dor Diavo loom in sight.

"Fish Catcher!" King raged. "There is the fish you are to catch. I order you to catch it. Obey me!"

He stamped on the metal body.

The thing croaked sullenly. One tentacle released the launch. But the other tentacles retained their grip.

"Obey me!" King snarled. He was for the first time in the grip of panic. His calm was gone. And now his voice contained the same harsh overtones there were in the voice of the Atlantan ruler.

And the robot obeyed him!

Reluctantly its tentacles relaxed their hold on the launch. Splashing in the sea, it started toward the approaching boat.

Dor Diavo saw it coming. He must also have glimpsed the man who clung precariously to the black hull. He shrilled a command at the man who was steering the boat. The launch swerved abruptly.

"Catch that fish!" King shouted.

The launch was close, so close it could not turn and dart completely away. A tentacle reached out and grabbed it. Another tentacle fingered through the air. A scream of mad pain split the night.

King never afterward clearly remembered what happened next. He was too busy trying to hold on to the slippery hull of the sea-going robot to watch what took place. He caught a glimpse of a mass of tentacles folding in around the launch. He heard wild screams of fear. He heard the screams choke off into horrible, gulping silence.

If Dor Diavo had had the presence of mind to order his men to lie quiet in the bottom of the boat, the Atlantans might have escaped. The robot would not have harmed them if they had been quiet. But when the first tentacle came fingering into the launch, Dor Diavo struck at it.

The blow, or perhaps the unexpected resistance, seemed to rouse a latent fury in the robot. It had been constructed to crush all resistance, to crush the life from anything that floundered and tried to escape. Here were floundering men. Here were men trying to escape. It had not been constructed to distinguish between men and its normal prey.

King saw it lift the launch into the air. With a crack that could have been heard for miles, it smashed the boat against the surface of the sea. It jerked the launch into the air again, twisted it, spun it, literally tore it into pieces.

Then it picked out of those pieces the one thing that resisted yet—a man. Dor Diavo! One tentacle seized him, lifted him high into the air. He beat at the ropy metal arm with his fists, beat hopelessly. Another tentacle came up toward him. The two caught him. One wrapped itself around his neck, the other around his feet. They pulled in different directions.

Dor Diavo's scream rasped into silence forever.

The sight sickened King. He knew Dor Diavo deserved exactly what he had received but he was still sick.

"Return to shore, Fish Catcher," he gasped.

The robot obeyed him. He heard the soft throbbing of a launch following them. Markham's anxious voice called out to him.

"We're going back to shore," King called. "Follow quietly at a distance so you don't attract the attention of this thing."

He rode the mechanical monster back to shore.

"THERE will be no resistance," Sonthia said. "Without a leader, the guards will not oppose you. Instead they will welcome you, for they had little liking for Dor Diavo either."

The three stood on the shore near the opening that led into the cavern of the Atlantans. Soon they would enter that cavern.

In the east the sun was rising, its rays glinting across the surface of the slowly heaving sea.

"For my—our—people a new day is dawning," the girl continued. "We shall be free again, free to live as we choose. And the Invisible Ones can now come out of hiding and teach us the wisdom of the past. For us it will be a new world. And we owe it to you, Don King."

"You don't owe me anything, Sonthia," he said. "I did what I could. Fortunately it was enough."

"Nothing?" the girl queried. "I owe you nothing?"

He looked at her. There was a tremulous smile in her eyes.

"I take that back," he said. "You do owe me something. I'm going to start collecting on it right now."

He kissed her.

"I'm going to continue collecting the rest of my life," he finished.

"What I want to know," Joe Markham interrupted, "is what was that metal octopus? What was it built for?"

"It was designed to catch whales," King said. "That was why it grabbed our ship and held on. Its cry, 'Kra—*kor*' means 'whale.' That's all it was—a fish catcher, a whale trap."

"Well, I'm damned," Markham said. "Why didn't I think that out for myself?"

Together, as the sun rose, the three of them entered the launch, entered the hole that opened into the cavern where the Atlantans waited, entered into their kingdom.

THE END

If you've enjoyed this book, you will not want to miss these terrific titles...

ARMCHAIR SCI-FI & HORROR DOUBLE NOVELS, $12.95 each

D-31 **A HOAX IN TIME** by Keith Laumer
INSIDE EARTH by Poul Anderson

D-32 **TERROR STATION** by Dwight V. Swain
THE WEAPON FROM ETERNITY by Dwight V. Swain

D-33 **THE SHIP FROM INFINITY** by Edmond Hamilton
TAKEOFF by C. M. Kornbluth

D-34 **THE METAL DOOM** by David H. Keller
TWELVE TIMES ZERO by Howard Browne

D-35 **HUNTERS OUT OF SPACE** by Joseph Kelleam
INVASION FROM THE DEEP by Paul W. Fairman,

D-36 **THE BEES OF DEATH** by Robert Moore Williams
A PLAGUE OF PYTHONS by Frederik Pohl

D-37 **THE LORDS OF QUARMALL** by Fritz Leiber and Harry Fischer
BEACON TO ELSEWHERE by James H. Schmitz

D-38 **BEYOND PLUTO** by John S. Campbell
ARTERY OF FIRE by Thomas N. Scortia

D-39 **SPECIAL DELIVERY** by Kris Neville
NO TIME FOR TOFFEE by Charles F. Meyers

D-40 **JUNGLE IN THE SKY** by Milton Lesser
RECALLED TO LIFE by Robert Silverberg

ARMCHAIR SCIENCE FICTION CLASSICS, $12.95 each

C-10 **MARS IS MY DESTINATION**
by Frank Belknap Long

C-11 **SPACE PLAGUE**
by George O. Smith

C-12 **SO SHALL YE REAP**
by Rog Phillips

ARMCHAIR SCI-FI & HORROR GEMS SERIES, $12.95 each

G-3 **SCIENCE FICTION GEMS, Vol. Two**
James Blish and others

G-4 **HORROR GEMS, Vol. Two**
Joseph Payne Brennan and others

If you've enjoyed this book, you will not want to miss these terrific titles…

ARMCHAIR SCI-FI & HORROR DOUBLE NOVELS, $12.95 each

D-51   **A GOD NAMED SMITH** by Henry Slesar
WORLDS OF THE IMPERIUM by Keith Laumer

D-52   **CRAIG'S BOOK** by Don Wilcox
EDGE OF THE KNIFE by H. Beam Piper

D-53   **THE SHINING CITY** by Rena M. Vale
THE RED PLANET by Russ Winterbotham

D-54   **THE MAN WHO LIVED TWICE** by Rog Phillips
VALLEY OF THE CROEN by Lee Tarbell

D-55   **OPERATION DISASTER** by Milton Lesser
LAND OF THE DAMNED by Berkeley Livingston

D-56   **CAPTIVE OF THE CENTAURIANESS** by Poul Anderson
A PRINCESS OF MARS by Edgar Rice Burroughs

D-57   **THE NON-STATISTICAL MAN** by Raymond F. Jones
MISSION FROM MARS by Rick Conroy

D-58   **INTRUDERS FROM THE STARS** by Ross Rocklynne
FLIGHT OF THE STARLING hy Chester S. Geier

D-59   **COSMIC SABOTEUR** by Frank M. Robinson
LOOK TO THE STARS by Willard Hawkins

D-60   **THE MOON IS HELL!** by John W. Campbell, Jr.
THE GREEN WORLD by Hal Clement

ARMCHAIR SCIENCE FICTION CLASSICS, $12.95 each

C-16   **THE SHAVER MYSTERY, Book Three**
by Richard S. Shaver

C-17   **THE PLANET STRAPPERS**
by Raymond Z. Gallun

C-18   **THE FOURTH "R"**
by George O. Smith

ARMCHAIR SCI-FI & HORROR GEMS SERIES, $12.95 each

G-5   **SCIENCE FICTION GEMS, Vol. Three**
C. M. Kornbluth and others

G-6   **HORROR GEMS, Vol. Three**
August Derleth and others

If you've enjoyed this book, you will not want to miss these terrific titles...

ARMCHAIR SCI-FI & HORROR DOUBLE NOVELS, $12.95 each

ARMCHAIR SCIENCE FICTION CLASSICS, $12.95 each

If you've enjoyed this book, you will not want to miss these terrific titles…

ARMCHAIR SCI-FI & HORROR DOUBLE NOVELS, $12.95 each

D-71   **THE DEEP END** by Gregory Luce
TO WATCH BY NIGHT by Robert Moore Williams

D-72   **SWORDSMAN OF LOST TERRA** by Poul Anderson
PLANET OF GHOSTS by David V. Reed

D-73   **MOON OF BATTLE** by J. J. Allerton
THE MUTANT WEAPON by Murray Leinster

D-74   **OLD SPACEMEN NEVER DIE!** John Jakes
RETURN TO EARTH by Bryan Berry

D-75   **THE THING FROM UNDERNEATH** by Milton Lesser
OPERATION INTERSTELLAR by George O. Smith

D-76   **THE BURNING WORLD** by Algis Budrys
FOREVER IS TOO LONG by Chester S. Geier

D-77   **THE COSMIC JUNKMAN** by Rog Phillips
THE ULTIMATE WEAPON by John W. Campbell

D-78   **THE TIES OF EARTH** by James H. Schmitz
CUE FOR QUIET by Thomas L. Sherred

D-79   **SECRET OF THE MARTIANS** by Paul W. Fairman
THE VARIABLE MAN by Philip K. Dick

D-80   **THE GREEN GIRL** by Jack Williamson
THE ROBOT PERIL by Don Wilcox

ARMCHAIR SCIENCE FICTION CLASSICS, $12.95 each

C-25   **THE STAR KINGS**
by Edmond Hamilton

C-26   **NOT IN SOLITUDE**
by Kenneth Gantz

C-32   **PROMETHEUS II**
by S. J. Byrne

ARMCHAIR SCI-FI & HORROR GEMS SERIES, $12.95 each

G-7   **SCIENCE FICTION GEMS, Vol. Four**
Jack Sharkey and others

G-8   **HORROR GEMS, Vol. Four**
Seabury Quinn and others

If you've enjoyed this book, you will not want to miss these terrific titles…

ARMCHAIR SCI-FI & HORROR DOUBLE NOVELS, $12.95 each

D-81   **THE LAST PLEA** by Robert Bloch
THE STATUS CIVILIZATION by Robert Sheckley

D-82   **WOMAN FROM ANOTHER PLANET** by Frank Belknap Long
HOMECALLING by Judith Merril

D-83   **WHEN TWO WORLDS MEET** by Robert Moore Williams
THE MAN WHO HAD NO BRAINS by Jeff Sutton

D-84   **THE SPECTRE OF SUICIDE SWAMP** by E. K. Jarvis
IT'S MAGIC, YOU DOPE! by Jack Sharkey

D-85   **THE STARSHIP FROM SIRIUS** by Rog Phillips
FINAL WEAPON by Everett Cole

D-86   **TREASURE ON THUNDER MOON** by Edmond Hamilton
TRAIL OF THE ASTROGAR by Henry Haase

D-87   **THE VENUS ENIGMA** by Joe Gibson
THE WOMAN IN SKIN 13 by Paul W. Fairman

D-88   **THE MAD ROBOT** by William P. McGivern
THE RUNNING MAN by J. Holly Hunter

D-89   **VENGEANCE OF KYVOR** by Randall Garrett
AT THE EARTH'S CORE by Edgar Rice Burroughs

D-90   **DWELLERS OF THE DEEP** by Don Wilcox
NIGHT OF THE LONG KNIVES by Fritz Leiber

ARMCHAIR SCIENCE FICTION CLASSICS, $12.95 each

C-28   **THE MAN FROM TOMORROW**
by Stanton A. Coblentz

C-29   **THE GREEN MAN OF GRAYPEC**
by Festus Pragnell

C-30   **THE SHAVER MYSTERY, Book Four**
by Richard S. Shaver

ARMCHAIR MASTERS OF SCIENCE FICTION SERIES, $16.95 each

MS-7   **MASTERS OF SCIENCE FICTION AND FANTASY, Vol. Seven**
Lester del Rey, "The Band Played On" and other tales

MS-8   **MASTERS OF SCIENCE FICTION, Vol. Eight**
Milton Lesser, "'A' as in Android" and other tales

If you've enjoyed this book, you will not want to miss these terrific titles…

ARMCHAIR SCI-FI & HORROR DOUBLE NOVELS, $12.95 each

D-91   **THE TIME TRAP** by Henry Kuttner
        THE LUNAR LICHEN by Hal Clement

D-92   **SARGASSO OF LOST STARSHIPS** by Poul Anderson
        THE ICE QUEEN by Don Wilcox

D-93   **THE PRINCE OF SPACE** by Jack Williamson
        POWER by Harl Vincent

D-94   **PLANET OF NO RETURN** by Howard Browne
        THE ANNIHILATOR COMES by Ed Earl Repp

D-95   **THE SINISTER INVASION** by Edmond Hamilton
        OPERATION TERROR by Murray Leinster

D-96   **TRANSIENT** by Ward Moore
        THE WORLD-MOVER by George O. Smith

D-97   **FORTY DAYS HAS SEPTEMBER** by Milton Lesser
        THE DEVIL'S PLANET by David Wright O'Brien

D-98   **THE CYBERENE** by Rog Phillips
        BADGE OF INFAMY by Lester del Rey

D-99   **THE JUSTICE OF MARTIN BRAND** by Raymond A. Palmer
        BRING BACK MY BRAIN by Dwight V. Swain

D-100   **WIDE-OPEN PLANET** by L. Sprague de Camp
        AND THEN THE TOWN TOOK OFF by Richard Wilson

ARMCHAIR SCIENCE FICTION CLASSICS, $12.95 each

C-31   **THE GOLDEN GUARDSMEN**
        by S. J. Byrne

C-32   **ONE AGAINST THE MOON**
        by Donald A. Wollheim

C-33   **HIDDEN CITY**
        by Chester S. Geier

ARMCHAIR SCI-FI & HORROR GEMS SERIES, $12.95 each

G-9   **SCIENCE FICTION GEMS, Vol. Five**
        Clifford D. Simak and others

G-10   **HORROR GEMS, Vol. Five**
        E. Hoffman Price and others

If you've enjoyed this book, you will not want to miss these terrific titles…

ARMCHAIR SCI-FI & HORROR DOUBLE NOVELS, $12.95 each

D-101   **THE CONQUEST OF THE PLANETS** by John W. Campbell
        THE MAN WHO ANNEXED THE MOON by Bob Olsen

D-102   **WEAPON FROM THE STARS** by Rog Phillips
        THE EARTH WAR by Mack Reynolds

D-103   **THE ALIEN INTELLIGENCE** by Jack Williamson
        INTO THE FOURTH DIMENSION by Ray Cummings

D-104   **THE CRYSTAL PLANETOIDS** by Stanton A. Coblentz
        SURVIVORS FROM 9,000 B. C. by Robert Moore Williams

D-105   **THE TIME PROJECTOR** by David H. Keller, M.D. and David Lasser
        STRANGE COMPULSION by Philip Jose Farmer

D-106   **WHOM THE GODS WOULD SLAY** by Paul W. Fairman
        MEN IN THE WALLS by William Tenn

D-107   **LOCKED WORLDS** by Edmond Hamilton
        THE LAND THAT TIME FORGOT by Edgar Rice Burroughs

D-108   **STAY OUT OF SPACE** by Dwight V. Swain
        REBELS OF THE RED PLANET by Charles L. Fontenay

D-109   **THE METAMORPHS** by S. J. Byrne
        MICROCOSMIC BUCCANEERS by Harl Vincent

D-110   **YOU CAN'T ESCAPE FROM MARS** by E. K. Jarvis
        THE MAN WITH FIVE LIVES by David V. Reed

ARMCHAIR SCIENCE FICTION CLASSICS, $12.95 each

C-34   **30 DAY WONDER**
       by Richard Wilson

C-35   **G.O.G. 666**
       by John Taine

C-36   **RALPH 124C 41+**
       by Hugo Gernsback

ARMCHAIR SCI-FI & HORROR GEMS SERIES, $12.95 each

G-11   **SCIENCE FICTION GEMS, Vol. Six**
       Edmond Hamilton and others

G-12   **HORROR GEMS, Vol. Six**
       Henry Slesar and others